The Lure of the Italian Treasure

Frank's stallion took off straight into a full gallop.

Joe's mare was right behind, and the cadence of their hoofbeats echoed off the hard stone wall in the hot Tuscan air.

Abruptly a gun blast erupted from behind the wall. Frank's hot-blooded and skittish horse bolted to the left, directly in front of Joe's mare.

"Steady, boy!" Frank yelled. He yanked hard on the right rein and dug his left knee into the stallion's side, trying to pull the horse out of Joe's path—but it was no use. Joe's mare was barreling full speed right for him.

The Hardy Boys Mystery Stories

Available from MINSTREL Books

157

THE LURE OF THE ITALIAN TREASURE

FRANKLIN W. DIXON

A MINSTREL® BOOK

Published by POCKET BOOKS
New York   London   Toronto   Sydney   Tokyo   Singapore

This book is a work of fiction. Names, characters, places and incidents are products of the author's imagination or are used fictitiously. Any resemblance to actual events or locales or persons living or dead is entirely coincidental.

A MINSTREL PAPERBACK *Original*

A Minstrel Book published by
POCKET BOOKS, a division of Simon & Schuster Inc.
1230 Avenue of the Americas, New York, NY 10020

Copyright © 1999 by Simon & Schuster Inc.

Front cover illustration by Broeck Steadman

ISBN: 0-671-03445-6

First Minstrel Books printing July 1999

10 9 8 7 6 5 4 3 2

THE HARDY BOYS MYSTERY STORIES is a trademark of Simon & Schuster Inc.

THE HARDY BOYS, A MINSTREL BOOK and colophon are registered trademarks of Simon & Schuster Inc.

Printed in the U.S.A.

Contents

THE LURE OF THE ITALIAN TREASURE

1 A Piece of the Puzzle

"Awesome!" Joe Hardy exclaimed. He was brushing away dirt and soot that had buried the ancient Etruscan pottery fragment for ages. "I think it's got something written on it." He stuck his five-inch pointed trowel underneath the fragment and carefully started to pry it loose.

Joe was working about five feet from his older brother, Frank, on an archaeological dig in a suburb of Florence, Italy, called Sesto Fiorentino. Joe knew that if the small black marks painted across the tan hand-size fragment were letters, they had to have been painted sometime before 500 B.C. That was when archaeologists had determined, using radiocarbon dating, that the Etruscan building they were excavating had burned down.

"Good going, Joe," Frank said. An inch taller than Joe but more slender, Frank walked over to see what his brother had found. "This could be important," Frank said after he got a look.

"No kidding," Joe said. "It's like somebody's trying to talk to us from a time before the rise of Rome—I mean, like, six hundred years before the Colosseum was built!"

For the past year Joe had dreamed of some day visiting the Etruscans' magnificent underground cities of the dead, which had once been filled with fabulous hoards of treasure from all over the ancient Mediterranean world. Now he could hardly believe—even after working hard all morning in the hot summer sun—that he and Frank were actually here sifting through the soil where the Etruscans had lived and ruled thousands of years earlier.

Joe wiped the sweat from his forehead with the large red handkerchief his girlfriend, Iola, had given him before he'd left the United States, three days earlier. She had said she wanted him to think of her when he made an important discovery. So far he'd used the handkerchief only when he and Frank had had to deal with a problem with customs in the Milan airport.

Now he took the sweat-soaked cloth and, without thinking about anything except getting a better look at the writing, started rubbing the fragment.

"Joseph Hardy, stop that at once!" came a perturbed voice from behind him. It wasn't the first time Julia Russell had yelled at Joe for unwittingly breaking the rules of the dig, but this was definitely the loudest reprimand so far.

Julia was a serious young Englishwoman getting her doctorate in archaeology at the University of Florence. She was in charge of Frank and Joe's section—what was left of one room of a small two-room house. Another mud-brick house with three rooms had been found about thirty feet away.

Frank, Joe, Julia, and a seventeen-year-old boy from Venice named Cosimo Giannotti were now on level twelve, six feet down from ground level in their room on the western border of the complex. A fire had at some point left a layer of charcoal rubble that first appeared on level ten.

Joe hadn't thought that a little sweat would hurt something that had survived twenty-five centuries of dirt and worms on top of a fire, but rules were rules and he understood that—now.

"It's okay, Joe," Julia said quietly as she approached from her section of the room, carefully picking her way past the artifacts laid out on the ground. She took off her cap and ran a hand through her short red hair. "I realize it is tempting to try to get a better look. Just remember that the conservation lab in Florence has special techniques for cleaning and preserving the fragments—and I don't think rubbing with sweat is one of them."

"But *look*, look what he found!" Cosimo said, moving closer. Like the others, he had been working from a corner toward the center of the forty- by thirty-foot room, and was now almost finished with his section.

Joe handed Cosimo the fragment. "It's got four Greek letters and part of a drawing," Cosimo explained. "Let us hope there are more fragments from the same pot." Cosimo's English was almost flawless, though he spoke with an accent. He had been studying the Etruscans since he was a small boy and knew almost as much as Julia.

"Can you read it?" Frank asked, peering over Cosimo's shoulder at the fragment.

"Well," replied Cosimo, "I can identify the letters, but I can't make out the word. I think it must be Etruscan."

"Which probably means," Julia continued, "that not even Professor Mosca can decipher it." Professor Mosca was Julia's supervisor at the university and the director of the dig. "Etruscan is completely unlike all other ancient languages of Italy, and scholars have been able to translate only a small list of its words. May I have a look?"

Julia took the piece from Joe and examined it carefully. "Very nice, very nice, indeed."

"Maybe we'll find the key to the whole language in this pot," Joe enthused. He knelt down and began digging for more fragments.

"I'm not certain about that, Joe. But do slow down, please," Julia said anxiously. "Before we go any deeper, we've got to get this section ready for the photographer."

Even when something exciting happens, Joe thought, we still have to follow the same old procedures.

They had spent the day before learning these procedures at Professor Mosca's multilingual orientation program.

The idea was to loosen soil with a pick and then carefully break it up with a trowel, probing carefully for artifacts. If something was found, the loose soil was swept away with a brush. Then, finally, the artifact could be dislodged.

Small fragments were caught by sifting the loose soil over a bucket with a sieve. Then the full buckets of dirt were raised to ground level and emptied out in piles.

When the six-inch-deep layer had been fully excavated across the whole room, a photograph would be taken of all the pieces laid out close to where they had been found.

The sun was now directly overhead, making the room they were in feel like an oven. "This place smells worse than Joe's locker," Frank joked.

"That's because it has your feet in it," Joe shot back.

"Well, here's one person who likes having the sun beat straight down into our lovely little hovel," Julia said, staring up at Armando, the photographer. He was holding a large camera mounted on a tripod.

"Buon giorno, signorina," he said, smiling down at Julia. He had a flowing mustache and a full head of wavy black hair peppered with gray.

She raised her head to Armando and said, in Italian, that they'd be ready for the shoot in five minutes.

"You boys empty the buckets and I'll get Professor Mosca, so we can show him Joe's find before he leaves," she said, heading up the ladder.

Joe carefully returned his fragment to the ground and climbed the wooden ladder to empty Frank and Cosimo's buckets. After dumping the first one, he saw Julia returning with the professor.

The old man was mostly bald, except for a wisp of gray hair on the top of his suntanned scalp. He and Julia were walking briskly, and Joe could see that the professor was excited.

"This is the young man who found the painted fragment, sir," Julia said.

Joe nodded and smiled, and was surprised when the professor asked, in English, if Joe's last name wasn't Hardy.

"Yes, sir."

"Yes, I remember. Very nice, it is. We have the same word, *ardito.* I like it very much." He grabbed Joe by the elbow and directed him to the ladder that led down into the room. "You to show me, please."

The professor went down first, and went on talking in his quick, animated way about Joe's name. "So, are you very brave and daring, as your name says? If so, I will call you Signore Ardito."

"Yes, sir," Joe replied, "but, um . . ."

"Now, where is the fragment?"

Joe steered the professor to the site where he had extracted his fragment.

Professor Mosca dropped to his knees and took out a handkerchief. He spit on the fragment and began rubbing away the dirt, just as Joe had done twenty minutes earlier.

"Is spit better than sweat?" Joe asked Julia. She had followed them down the ladder and now was standing close by. She smiled and shrugged, as though to say, "Well, he's the boss."

The professor began speaking excitedly to Julia in Italian, forgetting about Joe. Soon he and Julia had clambered up the ladder and were out of sight. Joe was about to ask Cosimo what the professor had said when the lunch bell rang. The small brass bell summoned everyone to the grand three-story stucco

7

building at the northern perimeter of the lush garden. This was the huge Renaissance villa where all the students were staying in a wing as guests of the owner, Count Vincenzo Ruffino.

Without saying a word, Joe started for the ladder. "Wait a minute, Joe," Frank said. "We've got another load of dirt to unload before Armando can take the picture."

Joe said he'd dump it, and climbed the ladder while Frank attached the bucket to the rope. Once up at ground level, Joe looked down and was satisfied that they had made the floor of the room a nearly flat surface. The artifacts, mostly gray-black potsherds of the most common Etruscan pottery called *buchero,* were scattered across it with Joe's find gleaming in the noonday sun. The tip of the iceberg, he thought to himself. Joe reeled up the bucket and then gave Armando the go-ahead: *"Va bene, Armando, vai."*

"Grazie, amico," Armando replied. *"Sarà una bella foto."*

Yes, thought Joe, it *will* be a beautiful picture. "Hey, guys," he said to Frank and Cosimo as they came up the ladder. "Let's get some chow."

"What is 'chow'?" Cosimo asked.

"It's what cowboys call food in Western movies. I guess all this dirt and dust makes me feel a little like a cowboy."

8

"Ah, Westerns," Cosimo said. "I love them. If only they weren't always dubbed on Italian TV—I never get to hear the English. You must teach me some more words, *va bene?*"

"*Va bene,* pardner," Joe said as they reached the grassy area outside the dining hall, where a croquet game had been set up.

They were in the dining hall now, having gone in through one of the large glass doors. It was a huge room with tall windows and three glass doors. All twenty students and a dozen or so of the staff could sit comfortably at the three long tables that were set in the middle of the room. Some were already seated, but most were still waiting in line at the buffet.

Joe concentrated on seeing what was for lunch. There was chicken, spaghetti with tomato sauce, and some kind of deep-fried vegetable.

"*Stupendo!*" Cosimo said.

Joe looked at Cosimo and smiled. "You said it, Cosimo. This is the life, isn't it?"

Cosimo straightened his tall, thin frame and took a deep breath. "I think perhaps so," he said. "Cooking as good as Mama's, but no mama to tell me how to eat it." His black curly hair and matching black-rimmed glasses added to his look of bookish intelligence.

Joe turned around and saw that Frank was back at

the glass door talking to the count's daughter, Francesca, who usually ate with her father in their dining room.

"What's she doing in here?" Joe asked Cosimo.

"I don't know," Cosimo answered, "but I think your brother might need our help."

"Just what I was thinking," Joe said as they stepped out of the buffet line.

Francesca was about seventeen and wearing blue jeans and a simple blouse. Her beautiful almond-shaped eyes seemed to be reeling Frank in.

Never very subtle when it came to flirting with girls, Joe walked over and planted himself right between Frank and Francesca and smiled at Francesca. "Now I see why Frank forgot he was hungry."

Francesca smiled back and looked down.

"Forgive my brother," Frank said, pretending to be more annoyed than he was. "He tends to forget his manners on an empty stomach." Frank politely introduced Joe and Cosimo to Francesca.

"So you're the one who just discovered the painted fragment," she said to Joe. "I was just coming to congratulate you."

"Thanks," Joe said. "I'm hoping there's more where that came from," he said.

"I *know* there will be," she said.

"Are you interested in archaeology?" Cosimo asked in English.

"As a matter of fact," Francesca said as Joe ushered them all toward the buffet, "I was the one who first recognized the Etruscan wall in the garden." She turned and looked around the room for someone or something, revealing the long, dark hair that hung down her back. "Ah, there he is. Bruno! *Vièni qua.*"

A short, tan, smiling man in his fifties got up from his meal and walked over to Francesca. "This is Bruno, the gardener, everyone," she said. "He is a genius with flowers—but he's not much on archaeology. Cosimo, ask him what he thought his digging had exposed the day he uncovered the Etruscan wall."

After hearing Cosimo's question, Bruno pinched his nose and mimed the answer.

"He thought it was an old sewer," Cosimo explained, laughing. Bruno then whispered something in Cosimo's ear. "And he wishes it had been a sewer. This dig is ruining his garden."

"*Sì, è vero,*" Francesca said to Bruno, nodding that it was true. Then she turned toward Cosimo and the Hardys and spoke in a low voice. "But it will all be worth it. My psychic has told me that she feels great forces emerging from the site."

"You had a psychic come out here?" Joe asked, hardly able to believe his ears.

"You are a skeptic, I take it?" she asked, challenging him.

"Well, uh," Joe muttered.

"Just wait and see," Francesca said. Abrubtly she turned and walked back outside.

"Weird!" Frank exclaimed, after she was gone.

2 Treasure Trove

"Come on, trowel, find something interesting," Frank said out loud as he worked down into his section of level thirteen. After lunch, and after his team bagged, tagged, and boxed the artifacts from level twelve, he spent the afternoon watching Joe bask in glory. Joe turned up piece after piece of what turned out to be a wine jug that Julia called an amphora.

"It's what the Greeks called them," she explained. "We don't know the Etruscan word for these vessels. As far as I know, the only Etruscan word we know for any type of vase is *zavena,* for a cup with two handles. The Greeks called them *katharos,* so you can see there's quite a difference."

Julia and Joe had really been hitting it off. She ooh-ed and ah-ed as each piece of the amphora appeared, congratulating Joe on his careful work. Armando was there, too, photographing each find. It was hard for Frank not to feel a little envious, although he was happy for Joe.

As Joe finished packing a crate with the pieces of the amphora, Frank ran into a rock that wouldn't budge. He dug around the contours, leaving it to be removed when the dig got deep enough. The soil was getting blacker with ashes as they neared the floor, and it was very dense and difficult to break up.

"Another few inches along this rock and I'll call it a day," Frank said. The sky was still bright, but it was six-thirty and there was much light at the bottom of the pit. Joe was covering up his section with plastic to protect it from the air for the night.

Then Frank realized that the perimeter of the rock was rectangular. He cleared off the top until there was a flat surface visible. He tapped it lightly with his trowel. Clink. It sounded like a metal box.

Frank restrained himself and finished clearing all around the box to about two inches down its sides before he cried, "I've found something!"

While the others rushed over—as much as they could rush while tiptoeing over artifacts—to see what he had found, Frank didn't take his eyes off the box. He was trying to imagine what might be inside.

He hadn't thought he had taken Francesca's talk about the psychic seriously. At lunch he had joined

Joe and Cosimo in making fun of Francesca for believing in that sort of thing. But now for some reason he found himself fantasizing about some great force lying hidden in the box, waiting to express itself, maybe because he had watched *Raiders of the Lost Ark* too many times.

When Joe saw the box he was more practical, if still unrealistic. He was thinking about the great mystery of the Etruscan language that he hoped his amphora would help solve. Maybe, he thought, the box contained a scroll written in Etruscan.

Julia, who was already extremely happy about Joe's amphora, was beside herself. "You two must be good luck!" She flung herself down on her knees, straddling the box and elbowed Frank aside. "I've been working on this site for two years and not found anything except mud-brick walls, rusted tools, and potsherds. Now, after three days, you boys are hitting the jackpot!"

Frank knew the box would have been found by anybody who happened to be digging in that particular section at that particular level. Still, he couldn't help sharing Julia's feeling that it was his luck that had caused the find.

Now it was Julia's turn to break the rules. She was picking and lightly scraping at the top of the box with her trowel. "I think it may be bronze," she said. "I know we should just cover it back up and wait till the

15

morning for Professor Mosca, but I can't help it." Her voice was going up in pitch, sounding more girlish. "Joe, give us some light."

Frank wasn't about to try to calm Julia. He didn't feel any more patient than she did. "Look," he said, pushing his face up next to Julia's, only a few inches from the box, to examine it under the beam from the flashlight Joe was holding. "You can see a crack right below the lid all the way around."

"Yes," Julia said, "possibly the lid is made of a different metal than the base, which might have caused a corrosive chemical reaction." She took hold of the lid and gave a gentle tug.

Off it came.

Nobody said anything for a good ten seconds. Then Julia closed her eyes and took a deep breath. "This is beyond belief," she whispered.

Joe kept the light shining in the box. A magic space full of bright, glowing objects threw the light back into his face.

"It's . . . it's . . . a jewelry box," Julia struggled to say. "Full of gold. . . . Bracelets, fibulae, earrings, agrafes . . . all in perfect shape. Nothing like this has ever been found outside a tomb." She peered up at Frank and Joe and smiled triumphantly.

"Yeee-haaa!" Joe shouted at the top of his lungs.

"Shhhhh!" Julia said. But there was no stopping Joe.

"It's a gold mine!" he shouted, loud enough for everyone in the complex to hear.

"So much for keeping this secret until we can secure it," Julia said.

The first person to show up was Francesca Ruffino. Without asking Julia for permission, she started down the ladder. "Papa, come over!" she yelled before her head was below ground level. "They've found something here!"

Soon the count was peering over the edge into the room. Next to him was a man in his fifties in a white linen suit and a wide-brimmed hat. Joe noticed that this man was wearing various pieces of gold jewelry. Instead of a tie, he had his shirt open to reveal a gold pendant resting on his hairy chest.

Students from the adjacent room came, and even Bruno the gardener was peeking down into the room.

The sudden intrusion of Francesca and the gathering of the small crowd up above shook Julia out of her euphoric mood. Before Francesca could get a look at the jewelry, Julia had the lid back on. "We've got to hush this up," she whispered, worried. "Joe, tell everyone you were just kidding."

"Oh, come on, Julia," Francesca implored. "Whatever it is will be perfectly safe here. Papa can put some guards on duty."

Julia hesitated for a moment, unsure what to do.

17

"Good then," Francesca said confidently. "Let's have a look."

"Well, I suppose we're not going to fool anyone." She bent down and carefully lifted the lid. "Feast your eyes, Francesca."

"But I'm afraid everyone else will have to stay out of the pit," Julia said with authority, addressing the crowd above. Everyone agreed and peered down intently as Julia removed the lid. Joe directed the light into the box.

"It's a pity the government will pay you only a fraction of what the black market would pay for something like this," the man in the linen suit said to the count, loud enough for everyone to hear.

Joe thought that was a pretty weird thing to say to anyone, and an especially weird thing to say to a count.

"Allow me to introduce my blunt friend, Signore Antonio Cafaggio," the count said to Julia. "Despite all outward appearances," he continued, with a smile and raised eyebrows, "he is an honorable man. He owns the best ceramics shop in Florence, and, if I am not mistaken, he is very knowledgeable about Etruscan objects of various kinds."

Signore Cafaggio bowed and removed his hat. "Will you be joining us for dinner this evening?" he asked Julia. "I should like very much to discuss what you have found so far."

"Thank you very much, sir," she replied. "But I've already got a date with my assistants. We're going to celebrate." She flashed Cosimo, Frank, and Joe a quick grin and then proceeded to cover up the box with a small canvas tarp.

Julia was obviously too distracted to dawdle in conversation. She quickly turned her back to the count and his friend and finished covering up the box. Then she changed her mind. "I'm not so sure it's a good idea to leave it here, now that everyone knows about it. On the other hand, it's going to take some time to excavate the fragile base of the box. And I don't think it would be wise to handle the jewels."

"You really shouldn't worry, Julia," Francesca said. "Nothing will happen to your treasure. Papa, can't you arrange a guard for the night?"

"Of course," the count said cheerfully as the dinner bell began ringing. "We'll have Gino stand watch." He turned to go. "Oh, and Francesca," he said over his shoulder, "your young man is here."

Joe was interested to see Francesca give Frank a coy smile and watch as Frank blushed slightly. She started up one rung and then backed down. She walked over to Frank and gave him a kiss on the cheek. "Congratulations, Frank," she said, and raced back up the ladder.

She was met at the top by a tall, well-built young man, who had evidently seen this last interaction. Joe didn't know what he said to Francesca in Italian, but it didn't seem very nice. Without waiting to be introduced, he took her by the arm and whisked her off to dinner.

"Nice to meet you!" Joe yelled.

"Can it, Joe," Frank said. "Let's help Julia get this place secure."

"Actually, I think I'd better call Professor Mosca and ask him what to do," Julia said. "Maybe we should get some lights in here and remove the box tonight. Hang on while I go phone him."

Joe and Cosimo began covering up the site with plastic while Frank seemed lost in a daze. Joe assumed Frank was thinking about Francesca and so was working out a good way to give him a hard time when Cosimo spoke. "I think the girl, she is trouble. Take my advice and don't bother about her, Frank."

"Girl?" Frank asked, amused. "What girl? I was just trying to figure out why the lady of our Etruscan house didn't come back after the fire to retrieve such a valuable jewelry box."

"Maybe she couldn't," Cosimo said.

Joe smiled at his brother's success at covering up his reaction to Francesca's kiss. On the other hand, maybe Frank *was* thinking about the poor Etruscan woman who had lost her jewelry box, and possibly her life. With Frank, it was hard to tell.

When Julia rejoined them, she appeared more

relaxed. She had been unable to reach Professor Mosca, but did reach the conservator, Ricardo Corsini, who was in charge of the conservation lab in Florence.

"Corsini wanted to have the box in his lab tonight," Julia explained, "but we agreed that it must be carefully excavated. We will also need to get several closeup pictures of the excavation, and Armando is gone for the day."

"Do you think it will be safe?" Cosimo asked.

"Well, Corsini made the excellent point that each of the villas in these hills contains dozens of priceless treasures. There's no reason a thief would single out this box. Plus we'll put one guard at the site. So let's go celebrate!"

After showering and throwing on clean clothes, Frank, Joe, and Cosimo waited for Julia in the garden on a bench in the shadow of an old, weathered statue of some mythical warrior fighting a three-headed monster.

"Hey, we should pick up one of these for Mom's garden," Joe said. "It would inspire her in her battle against the rabbits."

"Do you think it's supposed to be one of Francesca's ancestors?" Frank asked.

"Interesting idea," Cosimo said, studying the statue through his thick glasses. Despite Cosimo's interest in archaeology, he planned on becoming a doctor. Right then Frank could see Cosimo was practicing his clinical gaze. "It's obviously meant to be Hercules fighting Cerberus, the protector of Hades, but it is true that artists in the Renaissance would sometimes dress up their patrons in flattering disguises."

"Speaking of disguises," Joe said, "look who's coming."

Julia had apparently managed to break away from digging and studying long enough to do some shopping in the fashionable shops of Florence. Her leather skirt, silk blouse, and high heels—not to mention her makeup—gave her a chic Italian look.

"Where to?" she asked, sidling down on the bench between Frank and Cosimo. "I don't suppose anyone would be interested in Chinese. I could go for a change of pace."

"Chinese food in Italy?" Joe asked. "Cool."

The Chinese food was as good as any Frank and Joe had ever had, and it was fun sharing Julia's excitement about the archaeological site. Afterward, Julia took her scooter back to the apartment she had taken in Sesto Fiorentino, while Frank, Joe, and Cosimo took theirs back to the villa.

Cosimo had convinced Frank and Joe to rent Vespa scooters so that they could explore the area together.

The ride home was glorious. Warm moonlit air streamed past them as they wound around the hairpin turns of the road leading out from the noisy congestion of the Arno Valley. As they ascended the peaceful beauty of the Apennine Mountains, Joe was straining every muscle in his body to keep his scooter under control as he threw his weight into a turn at top speed. When he hit a patch of oily pavement, he lost control, and before he knew it had spun off the road. He flew over the embankment and down the mountain like a skier going off a jump.

When he came to, he could remember nothing of his fall. All he knew was that he couldn't move. He lay motionless while a siren filled his ears with a horrible wail that he knew was heading for him. . . .

"Joe, Joe, wake up" came the sound of his brother's voice, accompanied by a violent shaking. "There's a police car parked on the street right below."

"Huh? What? Oh," Joe sputtered as he struggled to wake up. "Wow, did I just have a nightmare! I dreamed I crashed my Vespa."

"Your brain must have heard the siren," Frank said.

Joe got out of bed feeling dazed but glad to be in one piece. He followed Frank to the window, where he could see the police car parked beside the villa.

"Look!" Frank said, leaning out the screenless window and pointing at a man coming out of the garden door. The doorway went through the massive spiked wall that abutted the villa and surrounded the garden. The man was running toward the two officers. "It's Bruno and he looks upset."

"Are you thinking what I'm thinking?" Joe asked, as the officers ran with Bruno back into the garden.

"If there was something wrong in the villa, they wouldn't go in the garden door," Frank replied.

"Julia's gonna die if somebody stole the jewelry box," Joe said.

"She's not the only one," Frank replied as another police car arrived with its siren on. "We didn't even get a picture of the jewelry box. It would be as if it was never found."

"Let's not jump to conclusions," Cosimo said. He had gotten up, too, and was looking out the window. "Maybe it is only an ordinary crime, like a murder." He smiled mischievously.

"Well, let's find out," Joe said.

They quickly dressed and raced out. Their room, along with those of the other students, was on the top floor of a two-story wing on the east end of the villa. The boys went down the stairs at the west end of the wing and through the dining hall, into the giant kitchen, and straight out the double glass doors into the garden.

Joe pushed open one of the glass doors, and they

filed out into the garden. The brilliant, crisp colors of the flowers and foliage in the early morning sun jarred them awake.

They ran past the tall hedge that bordered the grassed-in area toward the Etruscan ruins, at the south end of the garden. As soon as they rounded the hedge they could see the guard sitting on the ground, surrounded by Bruno and four officers. Bruno was kneeling next to the guard, untying the cord that was dangling from one of his wrists.

3 A Suspicious Bug

Frank couldn't tell from the guard's deeply tanned and wrinkled face whether or not he was in pain. He looked a little dazed. Instead of a uniform, he was dressed in well-worn trousers and a sleeveless under-shirt.

"He doesn't look much like a professional security guard to me," Frank said to Joe and Cosimo.

"Perhaps he's one of the workers who tend Count Ruffino's vineyard and olive grove," Cosimo suggested.

"How could a guy who works all day in the fields stay awake all night?" Joe asked. "I bet he fell asleep on the job."

Frank was about to try his Italian on the officers to ask them what had happened when Cosimo took the initiative.

"They say the guard remembers nothing," Cosimo reported. "He says he must have been knocked out, but there's no sign of an injury. Joe might be right about him falling asleep."

"Did you ask if they checked to see if the box is gone?" Joe asked.

"They said they didn't want to disturb the site until the inspector arrives."

Frank saw something in a clump of roses about twenty feet away that looked out of place. He walked over and saw that it was a small white handkerchief. He bent down to take a closer look and knew at once that it was a crucial piece of evidence. The cloth was dry now, but the smell of chloroform was unmistakable.

Frank was about to get up when an officer grabbed him by the shoulder and pulled him back, shouting something.

"Cosimo, tell them that we're used to police work," Joe said when he saw Frank being manhandled. "Our father is a detective, and we often help him out."

"No," Cosimo said seriously as he and Joe walked toward Frank. "I think we'd better just be quiet. I know the type. Let's hope the inspector is more civilized."

The officer finished scolding Frank, and the three boys began walking back to the villa.

"Is it really true that you have done detective work?" Cosimo asked

"Once you've started, it seems to get under your skin," Joe replied.

"Wow," Cosimo said as they turned the corner around the big hedge. "I am a big fan of American detective shows. I never thought I would meet a real live American detective."

"We're not quite real, Cosimo," Joe explained. "We don't have a license or anything."

"Well, if you've helped solve real crimes, you are real enough for me," Cosimo replied.

Frank saw Julia come in through the door that led from the garden to the street. With her was a woman wearing a dark suit. Both women hurried over to join them.

They had gotten no further than learning that the woman in the suit was Inspector Amelia Barducci, when Professor Mosca came running up from a different direction.

"Che succede?" he said, asking Julia what had happened.

"Non lo so," she replied, looking nervously at Inspector Barducci and then at Cosimo and the Hardys. *"Parla inglese?"* she asked the inspector.

"Yes, a little," Inspector Barducci replied.

"Good, then we all have a common language," Julia said, glancing at the Hardys.

"But what is the problem that we are all going to discuss?" Professor Mosca asked impatiently. "I am eager to see the amphora that this young man discovered yesterday." He extended an arm in Joe's direction.

"That has already been sent to the conservation lab, sir," Joe said. "But there's some very bad news, we think."

"What do you mean?" he asked, again impatient. "You *think* there is bad news, or there is news which you think might be bad?"

"The guard was tied up last night," Frank said, cutting through the professor's argument.

"What guard?" the professor asked.

"Frank here found something extraordinary after you left—a box full of jewelry—so Count Ruffino agreed to hire a guard," Julia explained. "I tried to get in touch with you last night to see what you wanted us to do. Signore Corsini and I agreed to keep it in the ground so that it could be properly excavated."

"So someone stole it. Why didn't you tell me in the first place?"

"We don't know yet that the box was stolen, sir," Frank pointed out. "The police were waiting until the inspector arrived to approach the site. That's why we *think* there's bad news. Very bad news."

"Well, as I am here," Inspector Barducci said, "let us proceed to the site."

Frank, Joe, and Cosimo followed along silently, while Julia led Inspector Barducci and Professor Mosca, amid a barrage of rapid-fire Italian and waving arms, to their room at the edge of the Etruscan complex.

Frank could tell from Julia's face as she peered down into the room from the edge of the mud-brick wall that there was in fact bad news waiting for them down in the shadows.

Professor Mosca was the first to begin the ranting and raving.

Cosimo translated the Italian. "He's just using a lot of words to say that he's mad at everyone. He's mad at Julia for not phoning him again later last night, and at the Count for not hiring a professional guard, and again at Julia and Ricardo Corsini for not hiring a professional guard."

"It looks like he's going to have a heart attack," Frank said, watching the professor wipe the sweat from his glistening head.

"I feel sorry for Julia," Joe said. "It wasn't her fault. I mean, I would have stayed out here last night if I had known the guard was going to fall asleep."

"I don't think she's really listening anyway," Cosimo said. "Mosca's just making a lot of noise to express his frustration. He'll stop in a minute."

At the same time that Cosimo finished speaking, Professor Mosca stopped yelling. He marched over to a nearby bench, collapsed into a sitting position, and lit a cigarette with a shaking hand.

"Boy, there's a health nut for you," Joe said.

"You know, the guard didn't fall asleep," Frank said. "He was knocked out with chloroform."

"How'd you figure that out?" Joe asked.

"The thief carelessly threw the handkerchief over there in the rose bushes." Frank pointed to the spot where the officer had interrupted his investigation.

"And you recognized the odor of chloroform. Very good, Frank," Cosimo the future doctor said. "They have stopped using this chemical in operations because the patient's response is very unpredictable. But I suppose it works well enough for a thief."

"It explains the dazed expression on the guard's face," Frank pointed out. "He was drugged."

Now Inspector Barducci was motioning everyone away from the site. "Move to the house, please," she said in English and then Italian. "We must question everyone."

"This is going to take forever," Joe complained as they sat with the rest of the twenty students, along with the household staff and the count and his daughter in a huge room in the middle of the villa. Only Professor Mosca and Julia had stayed at the site, to make sure the investigators did no damage.

The room was covered with frescoed wall and ceiling paintings of pink-skinned angels flying through wispy clouds. Not my cup of tea, Joe thought about the paintings, sighing in boredom. But they must not have been easy to do.

Frank noticed that Bruno the gardener was acting more and more anxious as the time stretched out. It didn't seem likely that the kindly old man could have been the thief, so Frank asked Cosimo to find out if he was feeling all right.

Cosimo ended up having a long conversation with Bruno. After several minutes, he motioned Frank and Joe to join them.

"It seems Bruno is now living a second life," Cosimo said. "In his first, he was caught embezzling from a bank. He spent five years in prison." Bruno didn't understand much English, but nodded sadly when he heard the word *prison*.

"So now," Cosimo went on, "he's quite worried about the police suspecting him because of his record."

An hour earlier the police had taken down all their names. Frank assumed they were now doing exactly what Bruno feared, checking to see if anyone had a record. So far they had been working straight through without coming out of their makeshift office to question anyone.

When Inspector Barducci and one of the officers finally walked through the carved wooden door, it was late morning. She stopped just past the threshold while the officer pointed toward their small group. As she started walking toward them, Frank assumed, and clearly so did Bruno, that she was going to bring Bruno into her office for questioning.

Instead she said, "Frank and Joseph Hardy, please come with me."

4 The Secret Passageway

Frank and Joe followed Inspector Barducci into the adjoining room, which had a long, dark table underneath a huge crystal chandelier. As the slim woman motioned them toward two ornately carved wooden chairs, she took a seat across the table. Frank studied her small, dark eyes for an indication of what she was thinking. He and Joe knew enough about American police detectives to have some idea of the range of their personalities and methods, but at this moment Frank felt completely at sea. He thought Barducci didn't look happy. Had she been told that Frank was snooping around near the site?

"We have just received a report," she began, her sharp features becoming hawklike as she worked hard to form her words in English. "It concerns the espionage equipment that the Milanese customs officials discovered in your bags."

So that's the red flag, Frank thought. That shouldn't be *too* hard to explain. In fact, though, he himself still wondered why Joe had brought the bugging device. Had Joe just begun to assume that wherever they went, they would get drawn to a crime scene? Or was he planning a practical joke involving eavesdropping? Joe had told the customs officials that he had forgotten it was tucked into the side pocket of his duffel bag, and that he hadn't meant to bring it. Privately, Frank had agreed with the officials that that was a pretty lame excuse.

"This equipment," the inspector continued, "could be used for police work. But of course it is also used by spies and criminals." She scanned a computer printout that must have come from the portable printer set up on the table near a laptop that was plugged into a cell phone. "And you claim you are detectives?" She smiled slightly and raised an eyebrow.

"Our father is the detective," Frank answered calmly. "Sometimes we get to use what he's taught us."

"And you planned on doing some detective work while working on an archaeological dig? A dig, I might add, where there were no crimes until two days after you arrived?"

Joe wasn't going to stand for the insinuation. "But we were the first ones to find something worth stealing," he blurted out. He was including his amphora in the stealable category, even though its pieces had been safely sent over to the lab.

"Which means you may have been lucky," the inspector said.

"Look," Frank said, trying to ignore the accusation, "I know you'll probably think I'm just throwing up a cloud of dust, but I still think you ought to know that the thief knocked out the guard with a handkerchief soaked in chloroform. And my guess is that he did it sometime between three and five-fifteen in the morning."

Frank watched the inspector close her eyes and rub her forehead.

"How did you figure the time out?" Joe asked.

"Well, there was a bright quarter-moon last night. The moon would have set about three o'clock in the morning, giving the thief the required darkness until the sun came up at five-fifteen."

"Yes, I see," the inspector said. "And we of course know about the chloroformed handkerchief. We have already speculated that you were nervously checking to see if it still smelled several hours after you used it. It would be a classic case of criminal anxiety. And of course it is interesting to see how carefully you have considered the position of the moon while you were supposedly sleeping last night."

"Hey," Joe blurted out defensively. "That's the kind of thing my brother knows. He doesn't have to *see* the moon to know what it's doing. Anyway, we were both sleeping in the same room last night with our roommate. Ask him."

The inspector began writing on a pad of paper. "You may go for now," she said, not looking up. "But you may not leave the villa without my permission."

Frank and Joe got out of their chairs and walked out as quietly as if they were at a funeral.

"Sorry about that, Frank," Joe said sheepishly. "I guess I shouldn't have brought that bugging device."

"You guessed right," Frank said sullenly. "That's really all she's got on us, and she's squeezing it for all it's worth."

"At least we can handle it," Joe replied. He watched an officer lead Bruno into the inspector's office. "I hope she's not too hard on Bruno. He's pretty shook up about this."

Cosimo was still in the same chair. "You guys don't look too good," he said.

"That inspector's a real fruitcake, if you ask me," Joe said. "She thinks Frank's interest in solving the crime makes him a suspect."

"There *is* a certain logic to that, Joe," Frank said.

"But I'm sure she'll come around eventually, and realize she ought to take advantage of us. In the meantime, I plan on keeping my eyes open."

"By the way," Cosimo said, "while you were in with the inspector, Count Ruffino's lawyer showed up and complained bitterly about the count being detained for questioning."

"They're gone," Joe pointed out, "so it must have worked."

"Yes," Cosimo replied. "But pulling rank like that makes me mad. Why couldn't he sit here like the rest of us."

"It makes *me* suspicious," Joe said. "Maybe he's got something to hide. After all, it was his friend Signore Cafaggio who was talking about selling the jewels on the black market. Maybe Count Ruffino thought it was a good idea."

"I don't know, Joe," Frank said. "This guy must have money coming out of his ears. Why would he risk it all for a few more million, or whatever the jewels are worth?"

While Cosimo waited to be interviewed, Frank and Joe went to the dining hall to grab a couple of the sandwiches that the police had allowed the cook to prepare. Then they went out into the garden to see if they could get back to digging. They arrived at the site just as two officers were climbing out of it. Julia was in the room, alone.

"Possiamo scendere?" Frank asked the officers, wondering if it was all right to go down.

"Sì, sì," one of them responded, indicating that it was okay.

"Thank goodness you're here," Julia said when she saw Frank and Joe. "I could use a shoulder or two to lean on. This whole experience has been devastating."

"It hasn't been too great for us, either," Joe said as he climbed down the ladder. "Inspector Barducci thinks we stole the box."

"Maybe you did," she said, smiling. "What do I know about either of you, anyway. For all I know, you're not even brothers."

"And for all we know, you're an undercover cop," Joe joked as he reached the floor. "But you're not going to get any information from me."

Frank stepped onto the floor and walked over to the place that had been pillaged, shaking his head.

"How much of the floor was still covered by plastic when you got down here?" he asked Julia.

"Most of it," she replied. "Just the section around where we put the canvas tarp was uncovered."

"Since you can't see through the opaque plastic, the thief must have known where to go," Frank concluded.

"Yes, that's what Inspector Barducci concluded. She went over the whole scene before the fingerprint experts got here."

"No wonder we had to wait so long to see her," Joe said.

"Were any of the artifacts under the plastic smashed?" Frank asked, scanning the floor.

"Just one, on the path from the box to the ladder," Julia said. "Apparently, the thief walked straight to the spot, took off the plastic and then the tarp, and dug out the box with a large shovel, which the officers recovered in the garden."

"Just one person, then?" Joe asked. He was listening as he settled down to working with his trowel near the site where he had found the amphora.

"That's what it looks like," Julia said.

"And these fine scratch marks—a broom for covering up footprints?" Frank asked, studying the ground around the hole where the box had been.

"Exactly," Julia confirmed.

"Oh, man," Joe said with a mixture of excitement and aversion. "I didn't expect to find this."

Frank, Julia, and Cosimo came rushing over. Julia bent down to take a close look. Frank could see past her shoulder, and there was no mistaking it.

"I guess we just found out why we thought nobody came back for the jewelry," said Frank.

"I think she came back too soon," said Joe, examining the five perfectly preserved finger bones emerging from the black, sooty soil.

"It does look like the hand of an adult female,"

Julia said, carefully examining the bones. "I wonder if the house was burned in an attack."

Nobody felt like celebrating over Joe's discovery of a twenty-five-hundred-year-old skeleton, even though it was a great find.

"It's kind of eerie," Julia said, "thinking that we must be the first ones to see this poor old thing since she died."

"I feel like we ought to give her a funeral, instead of picking at her bones and putting them on display in some museum," Joe said.

"And I feel like I let her down by allowing her jewelry box to get stolen," Julia said glumly.

"Look, Julia," Frank said, putting a hand on her shoulder, "you did what you could. In fact, you did what the conservator told you to do."

Joe spent the afternoon excavating the skeleton, while Frank searched in vain for something to take his mind off the loss of the jewelry box. Cosimo started to work an hour after Frank and Joe and found a well-preserved bronze dagger in his section.

When it finally became too dark to work, the boys helped Julia cover up the site. They were about to say goodbye when Frank saw Bruno the gardener approaching. He was grinning from ear to ear and speaking too fast for Frank to understand.

"He says he just discovered that someone has used some secret passageway recently," Cosimo said, "and he wants us to look at it. He thinks the thief may have used it."

Bruno began leading them all toward the east wall of the garden. They walked on a gravel path past the rows of intricately laid-out flowers, whose colors were muted now by the early evening light.

"Isn't it marvelous," Julia said to Joe, "to be able to finish a hard day at work unraveling the mysteries of the past with a walk through this gorgeous garden?"

Joe wasn't the type to gush about flowers, but he knew what she meant. At first he hadn't been sure why anyone would spend so much time and money on a garden. Now that his senses were soaking it up, he felt that that well-tended beauty somehow made the world all right.

As Joe watched Bruno lead them past the groomed order of the formal garden and into a section where large flowering bushes and trees grew in lush abundance, he couldn't believe that Bruno would do anything to jeopardize his place in this beautiful microcosm, no matter what he had done in the past.

They arrived at a little hill that had been built up in the corner of the wall, so that when you walked up it, you could see over the wall to view the fields beyond. Bruno brought them to the base of the hill, where an ancient-looking statue was holding a cup and smiling.

"Guardate!" he said, pointing to the ground at the base of the statue. Look.

Joe could see clearly that some large, flat object had been scraped along the ground in an arc next to the base. It looked as though the statue and its pedestal had been pivoted on an axis.

Bruno reached behind the base and pulled a hidden lever. Then he pushed hard at the base of the statue, and the whole thing moved just as Joe had imagined. *"Il passaggio segreto,"* Bruno panted, the secret passage.

Joe took his penlight out of his pocket and shone it down the shaft that had opened up. "Wow!" he said. "This is cool."

"Bruno says he's sure this hadn't been opened in a long time before somebody opened it last night," explained Cosimo.

"Let's check it out," Joe said. He started down the steep stone steps that were built into the wall of the passage.

"Perhaps we should inform the inspector of this," Cosimo said cautiously, but Joe was already out of sight.

Frank looked up at everyone and shrugged. "I guess I'd better see what he's up to," he said, beginning the descent while everyone else stayed behind.

"Nothing down here except this old broom," Joe

said as Frank joined him in the narrow tunnel at the base of the stairs.

"Then Bruno is right. The thief *did* get away through here."

"Let's see where this goes," Joe said as he began climbing up the steep stairs at the end of the twenty-foot passage. Frank was worried about disturbing evidence but not enough to stop Joe.

There was a trapdoor at the top and a large lever to the right of the door. First Joe tried to push the door open, and when it wouldn't budge he grabbed the lever with both hands and pulled with all his might.

"I'll tell you one thing," Joe said as it began to move. "Whoever got this to move was no weakling."

As Joe pulled on the lever, the door above began sliding sideways in an arc, leaving an opening behind it. The mechanism creaked but moved easily, so Joe shoved it all the way open. He was about to climb out into the night air when a bright light went on a few feet away and shone right in his eyes.

Now another light went on, and through the glare Joe could see the light reflecting off a machine gun pointing right at him.

5 Cosimo's Fort

Frank knew something was wrong by the way Joe froze. He had to decide quickly if he should stick with Joe or stay out of sight and creep back through the tunnel to the garden.

Before he could decide what to do, a bright light glared in his face and he had to freeze, too. Then as Joe moved slowly up and out of the stairway, Frank followed him. He couldn't understand a word of the Italian that was passing between a woman and two or three men, and the light in his eyes made it impossible to see.

"I have a bad feeling about you two," said the woman. Frank knew right away that it was Inspector Barducci. "But lucky for you, I checked out your story about your father teaching you detective work."

She said something in Italian, and the lights were lowered. Frank could see that they were in a small three-walled enclosure, and that a statue of the Virgin Mary had been moved aside by the lever. They had emerged in the middle of a small religious shrine.

"It seems Mr. Fenton Hardy is well known in Rome," Inspector Barducci continued, "which apparently means that I must try to tolerate your meddling in my investigation." She was pacing back and forth, but it was hard to tell how angry she was.

"And now that you have made a spectacle of discovering this tunnel," she went on, "we have no doubt lost any chance of surprising the thief should he decide to return."

"You mean you knew about the secret passageway?" said Joe.

"Of course," she said.

Frank was wondering how she would have known when she added, with a sly smile, that the count had told her about the secret exit.

"And how did you find it?" she asked.

"Bruno the gardener showed us," Joe said. "He seemed sure that the thief must have used it. And he was right." He told the inspector about the broom they had found.

"And I suppose you think that means he is innocent."

"Bruno?" Joe said, not having thought that Bruno might have been putting on a big act to make himself look innocent. "I haven't singled out anybody yet."

"Whatever the case," she said. "I will give you one last chance. If I catch you tampering with the evidence one more time, I'll have to arrest you."

The next morning Frank and Joe were having breakfast with Cosimo in the dining hall earlier than the rest of the students. As they sat there, it occurred to Joe that the room was so huge—longer than a bowling alley—that it alone was probably as big as the whole first floor of their house in Bayport.

"So, how does Count Ruffino afford a mansion like this? Does he make that much from his vineyard?" Joe asked Cosimo.

"I don't know," Cosimo said, throwing up his hands.

"What do you mean you don't know?" Joe asked. "You always know *something*."

"Well, of course," said Cosimo, pushing his glasses up on his nose, "we all know *something*."

"So what's that 'something' in this case?" Frank asked, smiling.

"Well, the problem is, I can't quite figure it out," Cosimo said. "Not many of the old aristocracy *can* afford to keep up these old ancestral estates, even if they do run a business. If they want to keep them, they often have to rent them out to a business, or to one of your rich American universities."

"Wait a minute, Cosimo," said Joe. "You're not suggesting that the count might have been tempted by our Etruscan jewelry box, are you?"

"Did I say that?" Cosimo's shoulders went up and his hands looked as if they were holding a loaf of bread. "No, I'm sure he must just be a clever businessman," Cosimo said.

"I don't know," Frank said. "He looks more like a . . ."

Frank's jaw dropped a little as he saw Francesca, the count's daughter, approaching. She was wearing glasses with heavy black frames like Cosimo's and a white terrycloth bathrobe with a monogram. She was holding a plate of bread and yawning, as she shuffled across the room in her slippers. She had a newspaper tucked under her left arm.

Joe turned around to see what had stopped Frank dead and was surprised to see what Francesca looked like this early in the morning. "Well, I guess this *is* her house," he said. "No reason to get all dolled up for the likes of us."

"Hey," Cosimo whispered. "I think she looks cute like that. I didn't know she wore glasses."

"Cool it, guys," Frank said. "She's coming this way."

Joe turned around and smiled. "Will you join us?" he asked.

"Oh, hi," Francesca said, slightly embarrassed. "Excuse my bathrobe. I didn't expect to see anyone so early." She set her plate on the table and sat down with a sigh, then reached up to push her unruly hair back behind her ears. "Anyone want the newspaper?"

"Sure," Joe said.

"I guess you could look at the cartoons," Cosimo said with a smile, just as Joe remembered that it would be an Italian paper.

"No, you take it, Cosimo," Joe said. He decided to stay on safe ground and ask Francesca what the news was.

"There *is* a modest article about our little problem with burglars."

"I wonder who leaked the story," Frank said, remembering how Julia and Professor Mosca had worried about word getting out to treasure hunters.

"I wouldn't be surprised if it was Antonio Cafaggio, Papa's so-called friend, who just happens to be robbing us blind."

"You mean the guy who owns the china shop?" Joe asked. "What do you mean, he's robbing you blind?"

Frank wanted to know the same thing, but he was puzzled that Francesca was revealing family secrets to them so easily.

"Well, not really," she said. "I guess I'm still mad

49

that Papa sold him one of our family heirlooms—at an absurdly low price. If my mother were still alive, she'd never have let it happen. But Papa is like putty in that man's hands."

Boy, this is family secret time, Frank thought. I wonder what's next. He was glad Francesca was being friendly, but this seemed a little *too* friendly. And she hadn't even started talking about her psychic yet. It looked as if Cosimo was right about her after all.

Francesca leaned back and took a deep breath. "I'm sorry," she said. "This must seem so strange to you. . . . But I couldn't keep it to myself any longer." She looked up at Frank and really did seem miserable.

"No, don't worry about it," Frank said. "Maybe we can help." He regretted saying that immediately— what could he and Joe do? And the chances were that the count had his own perfectly good reasons for selling the heirloom. Maybe he needed the money.

Francesca sniffled and kept looking at Frank. "Well, I did hear from the grapevine that you guys have worked as detectives. . . ."

"You don't think this guy stole the jewelry, do you?" Joe asked, interrupting her midsentence.

"Oh, I don't know about that," she replied. "I guess he *would* know how to get a good price for it."

"Maybe we should keep an eye on Signore Cafaggio," Joe said. "What do you think, guys?"

"It seems like a long shot to me," Frank replied.

"Well," Cosimo said, "if he did steal the jewelry, I can see how he might think a little publicity would help drive up the price. Not that we actually know that he leaked the story to the press."

"I could show you where the castle is that he uses as a warehouse," Francesca volunteered. "I mean, if you think it would help. We could take my car."

Not knowing exactly why Francesca was so suspicious of Signore Cafaggio, Frank figured it couldn't do any harm to check him out as long as they were careful. "Okay, I guess if we leave now we can get back to the dig by nine. If it's not far."

"No, it's only about twenty minutes away, in the Mugello."

"Let's go, then," said Joe, happy to be doing *something* to find the thief.

Walking on the ancient rutted path through the forest, Joe was the first to catch a glimpse of the castle rising up out of a field of tall grass. Its perfectly smooth exterior stone wall circled around a central square tower that rose about five stories above the hill on which it was perched.

"You could see for miles from the top of that," Joe said as they reached the edge of the forest and peered out onto the clearing.

"Let's hope nobody sees us," Frank said, studying the structure for signs of guards or cameras.

"Oh, I doubt anyone's watching," Francesca said. "I've often heard Antonio brag that no one could ever break into his precious castle."

"So what are we doing here?" Joe asked.

"I don't know," she replied. "You're supposed to be the detectives."

As they crept onto the path in the clearing, trying to keep their heads below the level of the tall grass, Joe noticed Cosimo studying the castle carefully and stroking his chin. "Okay, Cosimo, what are you thinking?"

"Giuseppe, my friend," he began, using the Italian form of Joseph, "I am doing more than thinking. I am *feeling*."

"Okay, so what are you feeling, Cosimo?" Joe asked impatiently. "I hope whatever it is will help us figure out what to do."

"Perhaps it will," Cosimo said with a smile. "But first you must appreciate what this place means."

"Go for it," Frank said eagerly.

"Well, before me, you see, there have been one or two important people in Italian history named Cosimo."

"No doubt you will break the mold," Francesca said sarcastically.

"I plan to. But tell me, Francesca, do you have any idea who built this so-called 'castle'?"

"Of course not. As far as I'm concerned, it's just an ugly pile of old rocks stacked up around Antonio Cafaggio's treasures."

"But you see," Cosimo went on, "unless I am wrong, this is one of the citadels Cosimo the Great, the first Grand Duke of Tuscany, built in the sixteenth century in his campaign to revive the old Etruscan empire."

"Cool, Cosimo," Joe said, "but how's that going to help us get in, if that's what we're going to try to do?"

"You see, this was not a medieval castle with a moat, but a gun fort. The walls were made thick enough to withstand an artillery siege."

"So we should obviously give up and go home, right?" Joe said.

"But a citadel like this, in addition to having those pointed and angled bastions you see at each corner, would have had gunports several meters from the bottom of the surrounding ditch."

"Ditch?" said Frank. "There's no ditch around this one."

"My point precisely," Cosimo said.

"I'm glad you have a point," Joe said. "Remind me what it is, exactly."

"This fort probably hasn't been used as a fort in hundreds of years. The ditch has filled up with sediment. Sometimes in these cases, you can find a gunport in the wall at ground level hidden by the brush.

They were made large enough for several high-powered guns, so you can often just walk right in."

"But wouldn't they have the gunports blocked off?" asked Frank.

"This place looks pretty run-down. Even the main entrance just has an old wooden door. Maybe they haven't bothered much with the gunports."

"Sounds like it's worth a shot," Joe said.

"No pun intended?" Cosimo asked, laughing.

"I hope it's just a pun," Francesca said nervously.

After finding cover in the clearing, the group used it to make a dash for the wall. Working their way through the dense, thorny vegetation that grew up beside the wall, they eventually found a gunport at ground level that was mostly obscured by tall bushes. After gaining access, it was an easy matter to find the steep stone stairway that led up through the thick wall. Not a single door blocked their way.

At the top of the stairs they found themselves in a room with a roof and doors that had long since rotted away. Through one of the open doorways they could see an open courtyard surrounding the central tower.

"How hideous," Francesca whispered as they ventured out into the courtyard. Cafaggio had constructed a modern building made of bright green sheet metal right next to the picturesque old stone tower. "I knew Antonio had no taste," she said with disgust, "but this really is too much. He's ruined this place with that warehouse, or whatever it is."

"If that is a warehouse, I guess we could check it out," Joe said. "It's probably locked up, though."

"Are you sure this is a good idea?" Cosimo asked. "What if we get caught?"

"Oh, don't worry, Cosimo," Francesca said confidently. "I'll just say we're having an adventure. Besides, my psychic told me last night that she's sure the thief is someone close to the family. Who else could it be?"

"Oh, no," Joe groaned. "You mean you dragged us out here because of what your crazy psychic said?"

"She was right about the Etruscan site, wasn't she?" Francesca said seriously. "And she's right about a lot more than you know."

"Look," Frank said. "Maybe we're here for the wrong reasons, and maybe we shouldn't be here at all, but since we got this far so easily, we might as well finish what we started."

Everyone agreed and began inching along the outside perimeter of the courtyard, watching for signs of people, but there were none. When they came to the warehouse door, they were surprised to see that it was wide open.

After waiting a few minutes for someone to appear, they made a dash for the door and got in safely.

Cardboard boxes and wooden crates, stacked haphazardly, cluttered the floor. Plastic foam peanuts, crumpled newspapers, and bubbled cellophane hung out of every box and spilled onto the floor. Immediately Francesca recognized her family heirloom, a small Renaissance urn, nestled in a box like an abandoned ostrich egg.

Frank watched as Francesca reached into the box. He was about to ask her what she was up to, when he noticed the light from the doorway dim. He looked up to see the heavy security door they had entered swing shut. The sudden pitch-black darkness made him feel as if he had fallen into a well.

6 A Rough Ride

As the echoing clang of the heavy steel door petered out, Joe fought a feeling of panic. He felt like a trapped animal. It took him a second to come to his senses and retrieve the penlight from his front pocket.

"Everybody okay?" he asked calmly as he shone the light on the door.

"Giuseppe," Cosimo said, sounding only a little stressed, "I think we may be in trouble."

"I *know* we're in trouble," Francesca said. Joe was glad to hear that her voice sounded pretty normal, too. It seemed as if nobody was going to freak out. "My dad's going to *kill* me, if Antonio doesn't first."

"The question is," Frank said, "whether somebody trapped us in here on purpose, or whether someone was just closing up."

"I do not think it makes much difference," Cosimo said. "We are trapped either way."

"But if no one knows we're in here," said Francesca, "we could be stuck for a long time. Maybe we should scream."

"Not necessarily," Joe said, shining his flashlight along the ceiling to look for a vent or other opening.

While Joe was searching, Frank inched toward the door to see if he could hear anything on the other side. He tried the handle to see if it was locked. "This door feels secure, all right," he said out loud to himself. He pressed his ear against it when he heard someone putting a key in the lock.

He recoiled from the door as it swung open, the light streaming in and dazzling him with its brilliance. By the time he could see again, he was being yanked outside by a firm hand and thrown to the ground. The others were soon rounded up by a large man in a blue lab coat and shoved to their hands and knees on the hard terrace pavement beside Frank. When they looked up they saw that Signore Cafaggio was standing above them, holding a gun.

"Francesca!" he said angrily. He walked over to her, pulled her up by the elbow, and asked what she was doing. *"Che cosa stai facendo?"*

Francesca replied haltingly in Italian; Joe and Frank couldn't make out what she was saying.

"All right," Cafaggio said to the three boys when

he was finished with Francesca. "You stay here while Francesca and I call Count Ruffino." They disappeared into Cafaggio's black sedan to make the call.

Frank tried to sit up, but the man in the blue coat grabbed him by the shoulder and spun him back down. Then he kicked at Frank to get him to lie down on his stomach.

Patience, Frank said to himself, resisting a strong urge to grab the man's foot and throw him. The man was, after all, just doing what he thought he had to do to restrain trespassers who outnumbered him. Frank simply had to put up with lying there in the dust.

As he thought about the mess they'd gotten themselves into, Frank couldn't believe that they had been stupid enough to let Francesca lead them by the nose into trouble. On the other hand, had it been wise of Francesca to trust *them?* Now she was in as much trouble as they were.

"Now, don't forget to look *really, really* sorry," Francesca said as she prepared Frank, Joe, and Cosimo to go into the count's study. "Papa's a forgiving sort, but he *does* expect good manners."

She must think everyone's a pushover, thought Joe. All she has to do is look at them with those eyes.

In fact, it wasn't so easy to explain to Count Ruffino what they had been doing in Antonio

Cafaggio's warehouse. The count was civil enough, sitting behind his ornate desk surrounded by book-lined walls under a high vaulted ceiling. But his icy stare said, I have never heard of anything so foolish.

He dismissed them by turning his attention back to the papers on his desk, as though they weren't worth his time. He had said only one thing: "I trust we will hear no more of this kind of behavior."

"I don't know about you," Joe said after they shut the door to the count's study. "I'd rather be yelled at and shoved around than have to go through that again. I felt like a worm in there."

Francesca was waiting for them in the garden. "Why such sour expressions?"

"Basically," Joe said, "your dad has perfected the art of making the other guy look stupid."

"Except it didn't take much in this case," Frank added. "All we had to do was say what we did, which *was* stupid."

"You know what," Francesca said, "I've got an idea."

"Uh-oh," Joe said, smiling. "I think I've got to do some laundry."

"No, it's not like that. I was just thinking there's not enough time before lunch for you to work. Why don't we go have a pizza together? It's on me."

"Sounds good," Frank said, a little cautiously, "but we ought to tell Julia what's up."

"I already have," Francesca said impishly, and grabbed Frank by the hand. "I know a great place right on top of Monte Morello."

The villa stood on a small plateau halfway up Monte Morello, on the outskirts of the little section of Sesto Fiorentino called Colonnata. Driving from there to the top of Monte Morello would not normally have been anything to write home about. Frank and Joe had already jogged the three miles there and back once. But the way Francesca drove, it was an adventure. Going faster than was safe on a flat road, she would speed up even more so that she could screech her tires on the hairpin turns. She gripped the wheel as if she were trying to wrestle it to the ground.

"Do you always drive like that?" Frank asked as they came to a screeching stop outside the restaurant.

"Excuse my brother," Joe said. "He's the only guy I know who's gotten a ticket for going *under* the speed limit."

"You can laugh all the way to your funeral, if you want," Frank said.

"Well, you know, you have to give a good car a workout or it won't be happy—just like a horse," Francesca explained.

61

"Do you ride?" Frank asked.

"Constantly," Francesca said as they came to the door. "In fact, you can see our stables from here." She pointed to a group of buildings and a ring in a clearing near the villa on the plateau below.

Beyond Francesca's private little plateau, Frank could see far into the distance, past the airport, the modern apartment buildings, and the factories of the Arno Valley. On the horizon lay the low-lying buildings of Florence, a dense cluster of red-tiled roofs dwarfed by the dome of the cathedral of Santa Maria del Fiore.

"I guess you know you're pretty lucky, living in a place like this," Frank said to Francesca.

"Yes, of course," she said with a sigh. "But I don't know how much longer our luck will hold out."

"You mean, um . . ." Frank couldn't think of a nice way to refer to the money problems she had hinted about at breakfast.

"Yes, Frank. I don't know how much longer we can afford to keep the place going."

"Are you sure it's that bad?" Joe asked.

"That's what Papa says," she answered as they entered the restaurant.

Joe couldn't quite bring himself to feel sorry for her. After all, in the big scheme of things, she would still be a pretty lucky girl even if her family had to rent the place out. And if things were really so bad, why did she have her her own sports car?

"Joseph is giving me one of those looks that my father gives me."

"Well, it does seem like you could rent your place for a *lot* of money."

"Okay, I see you are a thick-skinned American pragmatist," she said to Joe. "After lunch I'm going to show you something."

"Okay—I think," Joe said.

"Can you all ride horses?" she asked.

Joe and Frank nodded. Cosimo shook his head. "We Venetians ride boats, not horses."

After dropping Cosimo off at the villa, Frank, Joe, and Francesca walked the half-mile to the count's stables. Francesca whistled when they got close to the fenced-in ring and a beautiful palomino mare came prancing out of the stable, her white mane glistening in the midday sun.

"Meet Lola," Francesca said proudly as the horse came up and reached over the fence to get her muzzle scratched. "She was once a fine show horse, and she still has a lot of spirit."

Joe gently pulled open her mouth and examined her teeth. "She looks like she must be almost twenty years old."

"Very good," Francesca said. "She'll be nineteen

next January. But she still loves to be ridden." Francesca started walking toward the stable door. "Let's go meet your horses and get them saddled."

Joe ended up with a black Arabian mare that a friend of the family boarded there, and Frank took the count's young brown Hackney stallion. They started off walking so that Lola could slowly ease into her work. "She eventually does a pretty good canter," Francesca said as they passed an old shirtless man pruning an olive tree. *"Ciao, Giorgio,"* she called out in a friendly greeting.

He waved and flashed a toothless grin. Frank looked past him to admire the five or so acres of gently sloping land filled with evenly spaced olive trees. They were gnarled and twisted and grew low to the ground, as though they were straining to get away from the sun.

Lola broke into a trot, and Francesca led her up the slope toward an old stone wall that climbed the hill. The slope was covered on their side of the wall with grape vines, but the wall was so high that even on horseback Frank couldn't see what was on the other side.

Frank's stallion was growing impatient with Lola's pace and wanted to move out. Frank pulled on the reins and shifted his weight to signal him to slow down, but he didn't respond.

"You two go ahead," Francesca cried, seeing that

both Frank and Joe were working hard to keep their young horses under control. "Lola and I will catch up in a minute."

As though understanding what Francesca had said, Frank's stallion took off straight into a full gallop.

Joe's mare was right behind and the cadence of their hoofbeats echoed off the hard stone wall in the hot Tuscan air.

Abruptly a gun blast erupted from behind the wall. Frank's hot-blooded and skittish horse bolted to the left, running directly in front of Joe's mare.

"Steady, boy!" Frank yelled. He yanked hard on the right rein and dug his left knee into the stallion's side, trying to pull the horse out of Joe's path, but it was no use. Joe's mare was barreling full speed right for him.

7 A Smoking Gun

Joe's mare was just taking off into the airborne phase of its gallop when the gunshot made Frank's stallion bolt. Joe watched in horror as the stallion took a giant sideways leap into the path of his mare.

There was no room to maneuver on the narrow path, and Joe knew he couldn't prevent his horse from coming down on top of the stallion's hindquarters. Joe could do nothing but brace himself for the fall. He squeezed tight with his knees against the horse's shoulders and leaned down with his chest against her withers.

"Hang on, old girl!" he yelled as he put his arms around her neck and held on tight. She gave a frightened whinny as her front legs came down on top of the stallion's powerfully thrusting legs. Joe had a strange feeling that the tangled horses were falling in slow motion even though they were going top speed.

As soon as his mare's belly hit, Joe kicked his feet out of the stirrups and tried to direct his forward momentum into a roll to the side. He hit the ground hard, barely missing one of the wooden frames that held up the grape vines, and skidded on the hard, dry dirt. The horses came down the same way and Joe had to scramble fast to avoid being crushed by the twisting mass of his thousand-pound steed.

Frank's horse didn't have Joe's mare as a cushion and landed hard on its knees. It thwacked to a sudden stop, throwing Frank into the air before it rolled over. The ground seemed to fly into Frank before he could react. His face and chest were scraped across the rough surface for several feet before he came to an abrupt stop.

Joe jumped to his feet and ran toward Frank, but the stallion was up, too, rearing and threatening to stomp Frank.

"Get out of the way, Frank!" Joe shouted. But Frank lay there motionless.

Just then Francesca rode up and skillfully drove Lola between Frank and his stallion. She used Lola's muscular flank to shove the stallion, narrowly avoiding its hammering hoofs. Then both Joe's and Frank's frightened horses raced off down the hill.

"Is he . . . all right?" Francesca asked after swinging off her horse and running to Frank and Joe.

"He's coming to now," Joe said as he anxiously leaned over Frank. Not knowing whether Frank had broken any part of his spine, Joe didn't dare move him, though he was lying facedown in the dirt.

"I'd better ride down and call for an ambulance," she said as Frank groaned and winced.

"No . . . I'm okay," Frank said, slowly rolling over.

"Take it easy," Joe said, relieved that Frank could move.

"No, really," Frank said as he sat up. "I'm just a little shook up. I didn't break anything."

"You sure did a number on your face," Joe said as he examined the scrape that extended from one side of his forehead to his chin. "You must at least have a broken nose."

"Yeah, maybe so," Frank said as he ran a hand over the damage. "There goes my modeling career." He looked up at Francesca and then over toward the wall from where the gunshot had come. "What's with the idiot who fired the gun? Was somebody trying to kill us?"

"I'm afraid it was just bad luck, Frank," Francesca said, kneeling beside him. "A lot of people hunt around here—it could even have been our cook. You just rode by with the wrong horse at the wrong time."

"No kidding. That's one frisky horse you've got there."

"Yes, he's quite hot-blooded. But you were doing well with him, I thought."

Joe wasn't sure he wanted to accept this innocent explanation. He decided to climb the wall to see what was on the other side.

From the top of the ten-foot wall, whose large, uneven stones made it easy to scale, he could see nothing but a thin forest of deciduous trees with a path cut through it. He walked down the flat-topped wall several yards until he could see the clearing on the plateau below. As he was about to turn back to the others, he caught out of the corner of his eye a tiny distant figure running toward the stable.

He had a vague feeling that he had better start to play his cards a little closer to his chest. It was hard to believe that Francesca would plan anything like this, but he couldn't help thinking that if someone *had* tried to hurt them, he couldn't have done it without Francesca telling him that they were going to ride that way. He decided not to tell Frank about seeing the fleeing figure until they were alone.

I'm probably just being paranoid, he said to himself as he climbed down the wall. And even if she told somebody we were going riding and where we were headed, it doesn't necessarily mean she's involved.

"I'll give Frank a ride down," Francesca said as she rode up beside Joe. Frank was sitting behind her, with his arms around her waist, looking quite pale.

"Okay, I'll meet you down there."

As they rode away, Joe climbed back up the wall and dropped over to the other side. He searched the ground until he found what he was looking for: the spent cartridge from the bullet that had scared their horses.

Hmm, he said to himself as he sniffed the fresh powder. An 8-mm Fiocchi. That would be about right for hunting. He followed the path down, but found nothing else of interest.

When Joe reached the stable, he found Frank helping Francesca put up the tack of all three horses, the two renegades having peacefully returned home. He joined in, and together they began cleaning the horses' feet with hoof-picks and inspecting them for any injuries. They worked quietly, Francesca singing an old Italian folk tune that she said Lola liked.

While he listened to her singing, Joe wondered if she would steal to keep this life? And kill to keep her secret? Cosimo had said that according to the newspaper, the Etruscan jewels might fetch up to five million dollars on the black market. That could pay for a few household repairs, all right.

70

Having found no injuries that couldn't be patched with the first-aid supplies on hand, they were about to leave when a man walked in through the arched doorway. He acted surprised and, Joe thought, a little annoyed to see them.

"Oh, hi, Vito darling," Francesca said, running up to him and giving him a kiss. "You haven't met my American friends, have you? I was just showing them the estate when we had a bit of an adventure."

"I see. Inexperienced riders, yes?" Vito asked with a deep, thickly accented voice. He started laughing when he noticed Frank's face, with its scrapes and bruises.

"Oh, come on, Vito, don't be cruel," she replied, stepping back from him. He was dark and tall—taller than either Frank or Joe—and had a set of perfect white teeth, which made him look as though he belonged on the set of a movie. Joe figured he was in his early twenties. "Actually, they are excellent riders," Francesca said. "The problem was with Papa's new stallion."

"Perhaps he does not like Americans?" Vito said, flashing his teeth.

Joe studied Vito carefully to see if there was any sign that he had been shooting a gun or running down a hill. He did look hot, but then who didn't? It must have been about ninety-five degrees. Joe wished he could think of a way to get Vito's hand analyzed for gunshot primer residue, to see if he had fired a gun recently. But he didn't think he could get Inspector Barducci to do a nitric acid swab just because the guy was acting like a jerk.

"I'd like to see you ride that stallion past a gunshot," Francesca said, backing farther away from him and closer to Frank.

"Why shouldn't I be able to?" Vito asked. "How else does one hunt?"

"You've never hunted on horseback," Francesca said, laughing.

"But do you doubt that I could?" He stood there with his arms crossed, his jaw jutting out. He was obviously trying to look serious and important, but Joe couldn't suppress a snicker.

"Excuse my boyfriend's bragging," Francesca said, turning to Frank and Joe with a shrug. "I think he must be jealous of you."

Vito turned around and stomped off in anger. As Francesca ran after him, Joe shook his head. "There's one mixed-up chick."

"I won't disagree with you this time, Joe."

About two hours later, Joe was brushing the dirt from another pottery fragment when Bruno poked his head over the mud-brick wall and peered down into the pit.

"*Scusate,*" he said, excusing himself.

Cosimo looked up. *"Ciao, Bruno, come sta?"* He asked how the other man was.

Frank, Joe, and Cosimo left Julia in the pit to check out what Bruno wanted them to see. Cosimo explained it all to Frank and Joe after listening to Bruno.

Professor Mosca had asked Bruno to drain the large reflecting pond near the east end of the dig because water had been seeping into the trenches. Bruno had been unable to turn off the valve of the old pipe that fed the fountain with water from the reservoir on Monte Morello, so he had had to explore the extensive passageways under the villa in order to find the master valve.

He was holding the huge villa keyring, with its dozens of keys dangling from it, as he trotted toward the kitchen entrance. He seemed ten years younger as he excitedly explained what he had found to Cosimo. Whether or not he was making up a story to clear himself, he seemed genuinely enthusiastic to Joe.

"He says he's found a secret passageway that no one on the staff knows about," Cosimo said. "It's behind a set of shelves in the wine cellar."

"Did he find anything in it?" asked Frank, who still had a slight trace of a headache.

"Apparently nothing unusual. He just thought we'd like to see it."

"He seems to be in a good mood," Joe said.

"I think so," Cosimo said. "He even joked that now he has a place to hide if Inspector Barducci comes to get him."

"Ask him what our silence is worth to him," Joe said as they descended the narrow stone steps that led to the dank cellar.

Bruno gave Joe a dark smile in reply. "He asks how much your lives are worth to you," Cosimo said.

Joe realized this was a joke and took it as a joke, laughing and slapping the strong gardener on the back. But he could see from Frank's expression that they were both thinking the same thing. When a man who has spent five years in prison jokes about murdering someone, the humor has an edge.

Frank ducked to get under the beam at the bottom of the steps and was amazed at what he saw when Bruno flipped on the light—a large dust-filled cavern, teeming with racks of wine bottles from floor to ceiling. Most of them looked as if they'd been gathering dust for a long time. "There must be thousands of bottles here."

"It is no doubt worth a fortune," Cosimo said. "Suddenly I am not feeling so worried about Francesca—if I ever was."

"Well, the count *is* in the wine-making business," Joe said. "Maybe this is just unsold bad wine, going sour."

"I doubt it very much," Cosimo said.

Bruno led them over to the shadowy end of the room and trained a flashlight on the ceiling. *"Guardate il tubo,"* he said, tracing the path of a large steel pipe to a hole in the wall above a wine rack. The light traveled down the wall to a vertical piece of the framing that supported the wine rack. Bruno motioned them over and shone the light on the side of the frame. Joe put his head right up against the bottles, and could just make out the outline of a metal hinge glimmering in the beam of light.

Bruno reached behind a bottle several feet to the right of the hinge and pulled a lever. Then he grabbed a shelf and opened the secret door.

"Amazing!" Joe said as he peered into the dark tunnel. "Let's check it out."

After a low, narrow passage, a room opened up that looked like a little underground chapel, about twelve feet by fifteen. Eight simple worm-eaten wooden benches were laid out on either side of an aisle that led to a wooden structure, which looked to Frank like an altar.

"Weird," Frank said, turning to Cosimo. "Do you think some kind of religious group met down here?"

"It certainly looks that way. Perhaps the Ruffini were heretics at some point in their history."

"Hey, maybe this is somehow connected to the secret entrance to the garden," Joe suggested.

75

Cosimo shrugged. He looked as though he was deep in thought. Frank was about to ask Cosimo if he could guess when the chapel had been built, when Joe broke the silence.

"Hey, look at this chest," he said, shining his flashlight on the floor between two benches. "It's got Capitano Alfonso Ruffino marked on the top."

"Bruno says he's the father of Count Ruffino," Cosimo relayed.

Joe tried the lid and found that it opened easily. "What kind of uniform is this?" he asked Cosimo, examining a brown officer's jacket decorated with ribbons and medals.

"Evidently this count was not quite as independent minded as some of his ancestors," Cosimo said, bending over to take a look. "This is a Fascist uniform from World War Two. Captain Alfonso Ruffino was an enemy of your country and a disgrace to mine."

"No wonder the count hidden it," Frank said.

"Look at this!" Joe said as he turned back the uniform to see what else was in the foot-deep wooden chest. "A rifle."

"It must have been Captain Ruffino's weapon in the war," Frank said.

"Yeah, and it's someone else's weapon now," Joe said, after he bent over to examine the action. "It smells like fresh powder."

"Strange," Cosimo said, taking a closer look.

As Cosimo and Bruno heatedly discussed the gun, Joe kneeled down to get a closer look at it. He was careful not to leave or disturb any fingerprints as he read off the identifying marks on the barrel. "It's an eight-millimeter. Mannlicher."

"Did you say eight-millimeter?" Frank asked, remembering that as the size of caliber cartridge Joe had said he found near the bridle path.

Joe had told Cosimo about it as well, and Cosimo suddenly seemed to stiffen as he realized what it might mean. "So the person who tried to kill you hid the gun in here?" Cosimo asked. "Let's get out of here!"

8 The Black Market

Joe quickly threw the uniform back over the rifle and closed the lid on the box. "Let's go. Bruno, *andiamo*—quickly."

Bruno nodded and they all hurried out. Bruno waved them on while he secured the secret door.

"Wait a minute," Joe whispered, stopping after taking a few steps up the stairway. "I think someone's coming."

They listened as someone began descending the stairs into the cellar.

"We've got to hide," Joe said desperately. "If the count finds us down here, we're sunk."

"There *is* no place to hide," Frank said. "We'll just have to pretend we don't know anything about the secret chapel."

Joe steeled himself for the confrontation and began walking back up the stairs. He tried to trump up some excuse for being there as the footsteps approached.

"Joe, Frank, Cosimo—you down there? Time to stop playing around and get back to work."

"Julia!" the three boys cried in relief.

"What on earth are you screaming about?" said Julia as she ran down the stairs to where they could all see her. "You look as though you've all seen a ghost."

After reaching the safety of the dig site, Joe began explaining to Julia what they had found. Before this, he and Frank hadn't wanted to involve Julia in their hit-or-miss investigation. Nobody had asked them to track down the jewels, and what they had done so far felt more like bumping around in a haunted house than doing active detective work. Now Joe felt they were in deep enough to start in earnest. Frank felt the same way.

"I admit you've been getting yourself into some tight spots," Julia said after Joe had brought her up-to-date. "But I don't know if it adds up to anything but bad luck and lack of prudence on your part. You're fortunate that Antonio Cafaggio didn't have you arrested. And eight-millimeter rifles are as common as potatoes—my father even has one back in England."

"But why is someone—presumably the count—keeping a rifle hidden away like that?" Joe asked.

"I don't know," she replied. "Perhaps nostalgia keeps him from turning it in to the authorities, as I assume he ought to do. We certainly don't have any proof that he—or anyone, for that matter—tried to spook your horses on purpose."

Listening to Julia, Frank realized that archaeology and crime investigation had a lot in common, and that Julia would make a good detective. "So what would *you* do in our shoes?" he asked.

"I think I'd probably try to help my field supervisor finish her dig."

"No, really," Frank insisted.

"Well," she said, "I suppose I'd try to trace the path of the jewelry, maybe try to find out if there's a dealer in Florence known for working with tomb robbers and for smuggling ancient artifacts to Switzerland. But it would be dangerous and involve a lot of footwork. Definitely not something people in the middle of an important dig are going to have time to do."

"But, Julia," Joe said, "wouldn't you like to have the jewelry back?"

"Yes, and then there's reality," she replied, handing Joe his trowel.

Joe took the trowel and pointed it at the skeleton's hand, which seemed to be reaching for the missing jewelry box. "What about her? You yourself said we owe her something."

Julia stared a Joe for a few seconds. "I'll give you and Frank one day. No more."

"We're going to need Cosimo," Joe said.

"Okay, off with you then," she said as they climbed up the ladder. "And if anybody asks—I have *no* idea where you are."

"Okay, so we're in this thing for real," Joe said as they walked through the garden toward their room to change clothes. "What do we do now?"

"I've been thinking about Bruno," Frank said. "I know Inspector Barducci thought he might be leading us on. You guys don't think he could have planted that rifle in the secret chapel in order to frame the count, do you?"

"You mean, *he* could have fired the shot with Captain Ruffino's gun and then made it look like he didn't realize it was there?" Cosimo asked.

"If he did that, he's awfully clever," Joe said. "He sure has me wondering about the count."

"I don't think we're going to get anywhere without pushing some buttons," Frank said as they entered their room. Through the window, they could see an orange sun setting to the west. It looked like another clear night ahead. "How about we talk to Bruno? Find out what he knows about the black market in stolen artifacts. We can judge from his answers whether he's trying to hide something."

"Yeah," Joe said. "I bet he picked up a lot about that sort of thing in prison."

"*Va bene,*" Cosimo said, agreeing.

They found Bruno in the chicken coop, a ramshackle collection of crates surrounded by bits of mismatched wire fencing cobbled together. He stayed inside, feeding a hen, while Cosimo asked him questions.

It turned out that Bruno wanted to play dumb. He kept saying he was just a simple *contadino,* a peasant, and knew nothing about anything. He had no idea the chest was in the chapel. He didn't know who could have shot the rifle. He learned nothing about black market dealers in prison. He just wanted to be left out of the whole affair.

Cosimo was about to give up when Joe got an idea. "Tell him that we're going to have to report the gun to the police and that the count will probably be arrested for using an illegal firearm. Bruno will of course have to testify about his role in the discovery of the gun."

"*Aspetta, aspetta,*" Bruno cried. Wait, wait.

"He says he'll lose his job if that happens," Cosimo explained. "Maybe he *can* remember something about the black market in Florence, after all."

"Good," Frank said. "Tell him we need a name."

"He says there's an Englishman named Philip Speck, who is known to buy stolen Etruscan artifacts from tomb robbers. He says sometimes even *contadini* will find artifacts in the fields and sell them to him instead of turning them over to the authorities."

"*Grazie*, Bruno," Frank said. "And good thinking, Joe."

"So let's go check this guy out," Joe said.

"There's one more thing," Cosimo said as they walked away from Bruno and his hen. "Bruno says this guy is dangerous. He's pretty sure he's connected to organized crime."

"Then he must be the man we're looking for," Joe said matter-of-factly.

"Um, look," Cosimo said, stopping on the gravel path. He looked down at his feet. "I . . . I'm not so sure I should take part in this. Maybe it's better to let the authorities pursue this."

"You're probably right, Cosimo," Frank said. "But we'll be careful. Anyway, since he's English, you're off the hook."

Speck's shop was listed in the phone book, so Frank and Joe got the idea to call for an appointment. Joe made the call, posing as a rich American looking for a gift for his mother. After taking their scooters down the winding road into the center of

Sesto Fiorentino, they decided to take the bus into Florence, where Speck had a shop on a fashionable street near the Pitti Palace.

Speck was dressed in a blue sports coat and had a florid silk scarf stuffed into his shirt at the neck. Joe thought he looked as if he was in his forties, though Frank judged from the wrinkles around his eyes that he was probably a fit fifty. His shop was stuffed full of antique furniture, and paintings covered the walls.

'So you want to make Mummy happy," Speck said with a smooth, polished English accent. "You've come to the right place."

Frank and Joe made small talk, moving from piece to piece until Frank caught sight of an ornate wooden jewelry box that had a woman's face inlaid onto the top. "How much is that?"

"Oh, a very nice choice, indeed. You see that lovely face looks rather like a Botticelli, and in fact the box dates from the late fifteenth century, around when Botticelli was painting." He paused and rested his chin on the knuckles of his right hand. "I could let you have it for ten thousand dollars. And if you pay cash, well, we might work something else out."

Joe was wondering who would carry that much cash around when Frank made his move. "It's really tempting. I'm sure Mom would love it," Frank said, winding up before delivering his pitch. "Hey, speaking of jewelry boxes, did you happen to read about that Etruscan jewelry box that was stolen yesterday? I'll bet Mom would *really* like one of those."

"Come on, Frank," Joe said, immediately grasping what Frank was doing. "You'd have to know the right people to get hold of something like *that.*"

Frank could feel Speck's stare intensifying. He felt as if he were dangling a worm in front of a hungry fish.

If Speck saw the hook through the bait, he didn't let on. "Yes, wouldn't it be nice to know *those* people. But I hardly think Mummy would approve of such a gift now, would she?"

'You obviously don't know our mom," Joe said, shaking his head. "She loves that kind of stuff. She says museums take all the fun out of ancient art."

"Yeah," Frank continued in a complaining tone. "So she's decided to turn our house into a museum. We have to practically tiptoe around."

"Your mother sounds like an interesting lady," Speck said. "You know, I feel much the same way. I'm sure those stolen jewels are just screaming with delight, knowing that they'll soon end up on the pretty little neck of someone like your mother."

"She'd sure be proud if we brought those home," Joe said, hoping he wasn't laying it on too thick.

"Come to think of it, I just *may* have something of interest for you in the back room," Speck said as someone came in the front door, setting off a buzzer. "But first let me go tend to my visitor."

Frank turned around and saw Speck walk over and take a box from the man who had just come in. Frank had a sinking feeling when he recognized the man, who was wearing a blue lab coat. Signore Cafaggio's heavy-handed assistant looked up and made eye contact with Frank before Frank could turn around. "Now we're in trouble," he said to Joe under his breath as Speck and the man came walking slowly over.

"So," Speck began, "it appears you two have already met Signore Pino. What he has just told me leads me to believe that you gentlemen have not been entirely truthful with me."

Uh-oh! Frank thought. Another few minutes and we might have had Speck in the bag. Now he's got us. "That's right, Speck. But don't worry, I think we've got your number, anyway."

"I guess we'd better take a rain check on the visit to your back room," Joe said as he tried to walk past Speck.

"Ah, but aren't you curious about what Pino has brought over?" Speck asked, as Pino stepped forward to block the way. "*Aprirla*, Pino—open it, so that our young detective friends can see that you and I and Signore Cafaggio are innocent of the heinous crime they suspect us of."

Pino set the crate down on a table and ripped off the top. Frank and Joe obligingly peered in and saw a ceramic vase.

Joe stood there bent over the box, studying it carefully.

"Oh my, what a good little detective we are," Speck taunted. "You're wondering about a false bottom, aren't you?" Speck laughed. "But now you really have tried my patience." He turned to Pino and spoke in Italian. "Pino has kindly agreed to escort you boys away—rather far away, if you know what I mean."

9 The Dark Side of Florence

Pino, with his broad shoulders and long ape-like arms, grabbed Joe roughly by the elbow and shoved him toward the shop door. Joe jerked his arm away and then rammed it back into Pino's chest, sending him crashing into a high bookshelf, knocking it down and spilling all of its valuable contents.

Joe and Frank were racing for the door when they heard Speck's calm voice from behind. "I wouldn't do that if I were you," he said. Joe glanced back and saw that Speck was holding a gun. "You didn't think I'd be unprepared for the likes of you now, did you, boys?

"That's better," Speck said as Joe and Frank stood quietly. "Now I suppose we'll have to get 'Mummy' to pay for the damage you've caused. Fortunately, I know just the gentlemen to arrange such a transaction. All you have to do is walk quietly over to Pino's van and get in the back."

Speck spoke to Pino quickly in Italian, then slipped his gun into his right jacket pocket. He left his hand there as they all walked out the door.

When they reached the van, Pino swung open the rear doors and Speck motioned for Frank and Joe to get in. Frank bent over and put his hands on the deck as though he was about to climb in. But instead he shifted his weight to his hands and shot his legs out in a powerful horse-kick straight at Speck's gun hand. The gun went off and Speck went reeling into the busy street. A car screeched as Frank took off.

Joe swung around and gave Pino a punch in the stomach and then followed Frank onto the crowded sidewalk. They ran a block toward the Pitti Palace; when they reached the wide stone-clad piazza that slanted down from the prisonlike palace they looked back to see Pino running after them, his blue lab-coat flapping behind him like ineffective wings.

The lights were on in the big arched doorway leading into the inner courtyard of the Pitti, and people were lined up to get in. "There must be something going on in the Boboli Gardens tonight," Frank said. "Let's go in. I'm sure we can lose him in the crowd."

But Pino was running like a soccer player, unfazed by the heat that still radiated off the pavement stones. Frank and Joe ran past the line of people, jumped over a rope, and kept running into the courtyard. They had been there before, when Cosimo had shown them the sights of Florence just after they had arrived, so they knew that the garden entrance was across the courtyard. You had to give your ticket to a guard stationed in an arched tunnel that took you under the massive palace and out into the huge garden on the hill behind. The garden, with its paths winding through mazes of tall bushes, would be a perfect place to elude Pino—if they could make it past the guard.

Already, the guards behind them were blowing their whistles, alerting the security staff to a disturbance. But with Pino bearing down on them like a predator—and maybe an armed one—there was no stopping. He was in the courtyard now, too, closing in.

As they approached the tunnel, two guards jumped up and started shouting, *"Fermate, fermate"*—stop, stop. But they were unarmed, frail-looking older men, so Frank and Joe kept barreling on.

It wasn't until they got well up onto the hill that they were able to gain some ground on Pino. The moon shone brightly enough for them to be able to see when they were on a wide path, but in the lesser byways and in the tangle of the brush itself, they had to fumble along in semidarkness.

"I think we lost him," Joe whispered, panting. They quietly crept out of a stand of trees and looked down the hill. The Pitti was lit up, and behind it the whole city of Florence sparkled like a rich red ruby.

"Uh-oh," Frank said. "Now we're really in trouble." About two dozen flashlights were spread across the hill and slowly moving toward them.

"We've got to keep going," Joe said.

"But where?" Frank asked. "This place is surrounded by a high wall. Maybe we should turn ourselves in. We haven't done anything except run for our lives."

"Yeah, but it'll probably take a night in jail to explain that. It can't get any worse if we look for a way out."

So they climbed up to the top of the hill, where the old Forte di Belvedere stood watch, its twenty-foot-high walls providing an unlikely route of escape.

"I think I remember a place where a building butts up against the wall," Joe said. "Maybe we can climb up there."

They ran to the place Joe remembered and quickly got to the roof of the small add-on structure nestled in a corner of the wall. From there they found a patch of wall where the mortar had eroded enough for them to easily grip the large protruding stones and scramble up to the top.

"That was a close one," Frank said as they walked along the wall, picking their way through several couples who obviously thought this was a romantic spot. Exhausted, the Hardys stopped and leaned over the parapet to watch below as the search party arrived at the fort. One bright beam swept along the top of the wall, surprising the lovers. Frank and Joe easily ducked out of the way.

Frank scanned the horizon, wondering if Pino had gotten away, too. He spotted the huge replica of Michelangelo's statue of David, dramatically lit on the opposite hill, David's empty slingshot draped casually over his shoulder as though it had been no big deal to kill the giant. Callie ought to see this, he said to himself.

"Hey, Frank, you hungry?" Joe said.

"Starved."

They walked down the via del Forte di San Giorgio, descending quickly from the quiet hill with its beautiful stucco homes into the crowded, tourist-ridden streets of the historic center. They crossed the bridge known as the Ponte Vecchio and turned down the Lungarno, the street that went along the muddy Arno River, looking for a place to eat.

"Let's try this," Frank said, when they finally found a place that didn't look too expensive. It had the neat, crisp look of a well-trimmed yacht, with varnished wood trim around a large plate glass window.

"You sure we can afford this place?" Joe asked as they opened the heavy wood and glass door. "Look at the white tablecloths and fancy waiters."

"Probably not, but we can get away with it once, I think."

The maitre d' came up and looked them over from head to foot. Joe looked down at his pants. He had started out the evening looking all right, but after their run-in with Pino, it was a different story.

"Follow me," the maitre d' said with a stiff smile, evidently spotting right away that they were Americans. He led them to a little table off by itself near the kitchen door and across from the bar.

"Oh well, at least we're in," Joe said, sticking his legs under the table and trying to smooth his tousled hair.

"Don't look now," Frank said, lowering his eyes, "but somebody else we know just came in."

"Isn't this marvelous, Silvio!" Philip Speck said as he walked straight over to their table with the maitre d'. He stopped and held out his hand for Joe to shake. "You've found my favorite restaurant. You boys are getting to be more and more intriguing all the time."

Joe didn't offer his hand, but Speck picked it up

off the table and shook it anyway. "Now, Silvio, you must do your best for them. They must be very hungry. They have been running all over town to escape from a very bad man." He laughed and let go of Joe's hand.

"Yes, sir," the maitre d' said, smiling warmly this time.

It was strange. Speck hung around blathering about how sorry he was to have put them through all that, how you can never be too careful in his business, how funny it was to see Pino at the police station, and on and on, as though he hadn't just tried to kidnap them—or kill them, or whatever he was going to do.

He must not have his gun, Joe thought, as Speck pulled up a chair and sat down.

"Look, boys," he said seriously, "I'm going to level with you. I don't have anything to do with those Etruscan jewels—as much as I'd like to. If you ask me, you ought to be giving a close look to that count you're staying with. Everyone knows he's absolutely strapped, and I can tell you confidentially that he is in big trouble with one of his creditors. If I were he, I would rather steal than be in the kind of trouble he's in."

He knows more about us than he let on, Frank thought as he gave Speck a cold stare.

"Well, I'll let you boys enjoy your time here." He

got up and Silvio escorted him to a table in the other room.

As much as they wanted to dismiss Speck's information about the count being in trouble with some cutthroat loan shark, neither Frank nor Joe could get it out of their heads. But they didn't talk about the case until they were on the bus going home. In fact, they hadn't talked about much of anything while they were in Speck's favorite restaurant. Every time someone opened the door, they expected Pino to come crashing in. And then when the food came, they forgot about everything else.

"Obviously," said Frank, after the crowd on the bus had thinned out and they were able to get seats, "if Speck is the conduit for the jewelry, he'll want to frame somebody like the count."

"So," Joe said, looking around to see if anyone left on the bus might be following them, "we should be thinking that the count is probably innocent."

"Unless Speck is innocent and really is giving us a tip."

Joe buried his head in his hands and tried to sort it all out. "It's hard to think of a crook like Speck as being innocent, but I guess it's possible he just missed this one. Maybe there's some other dealer in town we should check out."

"I'm not sure I can deal with that right now," Frank punned.

"Two points, Frank. But you know what they say. You've got to play the hand you're dealt."

By the time Frank and Joe retrieved their scooters in Sesto Fiorentino, it was midnight, and they were ready for bed. They wished their underpowered rental motors could take them up the hill faster, but they had to be satisfied to putter up the road to Colonnata, past the building with the spring-fed horse trough built into its wall, and on up Monte Morello to the villa while the cars whooshed past them. About a half-mile from the villa, on a straight-away leading to a hairpin curve, they realized the car behind them wasn't passing. Its brights flicked on, and a blinding reflection filled their sideview mirrors.

"All right, already, go ahead and pass," Joe yelled into the night air. But instead the car eased forward to within inches of their rear wheels.

"He's trying to run us over!" Joe shouted as the car revved its engine.

10 Fire and Brimstone

With the car's engine roaring behind him and the glare blinding him, Joe struggled to keep his Vespa on track. He reached over to swivel the mirror so he could see. Then, in the wide beam of bright lights he could make out a path that crossed the road just before the curve and rose up the mountain on the right.

"Head for the path!" he yelled to Frank as he held tight to the handlebars and prepared for a rough ride. He was on Frank's left and couldn't make the move before Frank did, so he waited as the path approached, hoping Frank had heard him. The straightaway was fairly level, and as they pushed their engines to try to stay ahead of the car, they reached about sixty kilometers per hour. It wasn't going to be easy to jump off the road—if they were going to do it. Now the car was honking its horn and swerving back and forth, its tires screeching.

Just as Joe was about to give up hope that Frank had understood, and they were almost into the curve, Frank pulled off to the right. His timing was perfect. The driver reacted quickly by veering to the right and cutting off Joe's escape. Making a split-second decision, Joe turned left and applied the brakes at the same time. The black sedan whizzed past. Joe had to stick out his foot to stay upright during the skid, and he could feel the heat of the friction through the sole of his shoe as he slid over the pavement. Regaining control, he peeled off to join Frank on the path.

Following Frank's lead, Joe flipped off his lights and navigated by the moonlight. The car stopped and backed up. But there was no way a car could negotiate that narrow, rocky path. They listened as the car screeched off.

The path climbed up through an olive grove, and Frank and Joe kept going till they reached a clearing on the hill. From there they could see the road below snaking up the mountain toward the villa. And at the limit of their view they saw the villa itself, its red-tiled roof lapping up the light of the moon.

"Hey, the car just stopped at the villa," Frank said.

"And someone's getting picked up there." Joe strained without success to see who it might be, and then the car sped off toward the summit of Monte Morello.

They decided to head back to the villa even though whoever had followed them up the hill might return.

"I say we wake up Francesca and tell her what's happened," Frank said as he unlocked the garden door. "Maybe she can convince her father to search the house to see who's missing."

"What if it's somebody who isn't staying here?"

"Well, then, at least we'll know that it's not Bruno, or . . ."

"Or the count himself?" Joe asked.

They weren't sure which room was Francesca's, but they knew where the family apartments were and had heard her say her room overlooked the garden.

"One good thing about creeping around a house like this," Joe said as they climbed the stone steps, "is that the floors don't creak." Joe was wondering whether the rifle was still in the chapel when they reached the hallway and saw a light on in one of the rooms. The door was ajar, so they approached it cautiously.

Seeing the pastels of the walls and draperies through the crack, Frank assumed that the room was Francesca's. He tapped lightly at the door, and when no one answered he gently pushed it open. Thinking that Francesca might have nodded off while reading, he poked his head in and looked around.

"Maybe she's in the bathroom," Joe suggested, noticing a tiled room coming off the far corner. "I mean, maybe it's not too cool for us to be here right now, Frank."

"Yeah, maybe you're right, but I'm not worried about being cool right now, are you?" He walked in and called out Francesca's name, but there was no response.

"Strange," Frank said as he looked around the room. "I wonder where she is."

"I don't know, but let's get out of here."

Neither Joe nor Frank shied away from concluding that Francesca might have been the one who had been picked up outside the villa, but neither of them said it. As they were leaving, Frank noticed a butterfly collection mounted on the wall over the bed.

"Hey, Joe," he said, "you remember our butterfly collection?"

"Yeah, sure—but let's get going, Frank."

"You remember what chemical we used to knock 'em out?"

"Not really—something that smelled bad, that's for sure."

Frank was about to tell him that it was chloroform, the same thing the thief had used to knock out the guard, when a voice startled them.

"Francesca? Is that you?"

The door swung open before Frank and Joe had a chance to hide. The light swept into the dark hall and fell across the angry face of the count.

"What is the meaning of this?" he asked. He looked less imposing in his bathrobe, and the harsh light made him appear older. "Where is Francesca?"

"We don't know," Joe answered.

"We were trying to get her to help us figure out who just tried to kill us," Frank said.

The count walked slowly toward them, his jaw jutting out as he surveyed the room. "Let me tell you something," he said sternly. "I have no idea what is causing you and your reckless ways to disrupt our lives. But I know one thing." He looked into the bathroom and then walked over to within an inch of Frank. "Tonight it is going to end. You are no longer welcome here. Now please tell me where my—"

"Hello, Papa," Francesca said breathlessly as she walked into the room. Her cheeks were flushed, but her eyes still had their steady gaze. "What's everybody doing here?"

"Where have *you* been, young lady?" the count asked with a look that wavered between anger and relief.

"Just out for a walk in the garden," she said. "It's a lovely night and I couldn't sleep." She looked at her father in his bathrobe, practically standing on top of

Frank, and smiled. "I guess nobody else could sleep, either. It's nice that you all thought of coming here."

The count backed off, his mood obviously softened by Francesca's calm gaze. "Look here," he said, thrusting his hands in his bathrobe pockets and looking at Frank. "What's all this about being nearly killed? Is this another of your pranks?"

"No, sir, we were just riding home on our scooters, and someone tried to run us over."

"I see. And you thought Francesca could somehow help?"

Frank could see that the count was skeptical, but he went on anyway. "It's only because we saw the car stop here and pick someone up."

"Ah, but you see, a great many of the local folk use our villa, with its well-lit facade, as a rendezvous point. You no doubt simply ran into a spirited youth on a joy ride. Now, I suggest we all get to bed and try from now on to avoid letting our imaginations become overheated."

The count then calmly escorted the Hardys into the hall. They stood in front of a large casement window that opened out into the street, and he put his hands on both of their shoulders, as though to say, "never mind about what I said earlier."

After they'd said good night, a loud crash followed by the sound of glass breaking on the pavement outside shattered the quiet. Then the squealing tires of a car could be heard on the street. Frank quickly rushed to the window to look out. A black sedan was hurtling down the road toward Colonnata. Frank was pretty sure it was the same one that had chased them.

The Hardys, the count, and Francesca ran down the steps toward the section of the villa where the sound had come from—toward the east wing, where the students were staying. When they reached the stairs leading up to their hallway, they could see that the lights were on and heard people screaming.

Joe bounded up the stairs first. After a few steps he could smell smoke and hear people yelling "Fire!" in several languages. He had a bad feeling as he reached the top and looked down the hall. Smoke was billowing out of their room. "Cosimo!" he yelled as he raced down the hall.

11 Vito's Bad Vibes

Joe rushed through the narrow passage, against the stream of anxious students trying to escape the fire. Dense, black, foul-smelling smoke poured out of their room continuously.

It seemed strange at first that a stone and stucco building could have caught fire so quickly. The only exposed wood consisted of the ancient, hand-sawed beams laid across the ceiling. They were blackened by time, however, and Joe realized that they were therefore extremely dry and flammable. And there was the furniture. If someone had thrown a Molotov cocktail through the window, the burning gasoline could easily have ignited a bed and from there the fire could spread to the ceiling.

Joe dropped to his stomach and crept under the

cloud toward the doorway, hoping to see whether Cosimo was trapped in the room. He had about a foot of clear air along the floor so he kept on creeping, calling for Cosimo.

"I'm okay, Joe," Cosimo finally yelled from down the hall. "You'd better get out of there."

Joe had made it into the room and could already see what he'd half-expected. There was no fire—only a metal canister spewing out noxious gases and showing no sign of letting up.

"It's only a smoke-bomb," Joe yelled back to the others. He began crawling out of the room, only to find himself under a deluge of water under high pressure. "Hey, turn it off!" he shouted as a steady stream of water arched in through the window. "Tell them to turn it off!"

The water kept pouring in, and Joe realized that if it didn't stop soon, the building would suffer almost as much damage from the water as a fire might have caused. He grabbed a towel from a nearby chair, held his breath, and reached for the smoke-bomb. Still holding his breath and pointing the bomb away from him, he ran for the window while dodging the stream of water. A quick toss and the thing flew out of the window like a jet with bad exhaust. Seconds later the hose stopped.

"Well done, young man!" cried the count as he stepped gingerly over the slippery terra-cotta floor toward Joe. He was bent over to avoid the black cloud that still filled the upper half of the room. He started to slip and Joe quickly grabbed him by the upper arm. Fighting to keep his balance, he helped the count out into the hallway.

"Thank goodness you're okay!" Francesca said, putting an arm around Joe as they moved down the hall away from the smoke and water. "I guess it looks like somebody really is trying to scare you—if not worse."

"In that case, I'm glad this happened," Joe replied. "I was beginning to wonder if everybody thought *we* were the cause of all the trouble."

"I must confess, it did cross my mind," the count said.

That's an understatement, Frank said to himself.

"Well, you'll have to tell me all about what you've been up to." The count seemed to be more than relieved that there had been no fire. He turned to Cosimo with concern. "You must have thought you'd been thrown into Dante's inferno."

"Yes, sir, I did," Cosimo replied. He was still pale and spoke very softly.

Joe had seen painted depictions of the great Florentine poet Dante's Inferno, with its grisly images of the torments of hell. He hadn't read the book, but he thought a conversation with a count called for him to say something impressive. The statue in the garden of Hercules fighting Cerberus at the gates of hell was all that came to mind.

"It's a good thing Cerberon didn't get thrown through the window."

Everyone laughed politely, but the count appeared to be puzzled.

"I think you mean Cerberus, Giuseppe," Cosimo said, smiling.

"Whatever," Joe said, embarrassed. "You knew what I meant—the monster Hercules is fighting out in the garden. "

"On the contrary," the count said. "I had forgotten the name of that creature entirely, and I thank you for reminding me." He turned to Francesca. "You know, princess, I think I'm going to like your new friends. Now let's get Giuseppe some fresh clothes and call Inspector Barducci. We'll probably have to wake her up, but I think the situation is serious enough to warrant it."

After getting cleaned up and changed into some clothes he borrowed from a Swedish student—all of his and Frank's having been ruined—Joe joined the others in the count's apartment.

"Well, Joseph, do come in," the count said. "Now that I have found out a little about you and your brother, I must say I am impressed—certainly more so than Inspector Barducci seemed to be." He chuckled cheerfully and indicated a chair for Joe to

107

take next to Frank's, in what must have been the count's private living room. Francesca had apparently gone to bed, but Cosimo was sitting on the other side of Frank, and he looked as if he had recovered completely. "Please accept my apologies for not understanding what you have been trying to do."

"*Trying* is right," said Joe. "I don't think we've succeeded at all."

"On the contrary," said the count. "As we've just been discussing, it seems that you and Frank have managed to draw some very nasty characters out of the woodwork."

Joe wasn't sure if the count was including his friend Signore Cafaggio in the same category as Speck, and he also had no idea whether the matter of the mysterious rifle had been cleared up. He glanced at Frank, who subtly shook his head, as though to say, Careful, man—we're not home yet.

Joe took a chance. "So you think we were being chased by one of Speck's henchmen, and that one of them also threw the smoke bomb to scare us off."

"Quite possibly—yes," he said as a bell rang downstairs. "That will be the inspector. Let's find out what she thinks about all this."

When they had last seen the inspector, Frank and Joe had promised not to meddle with any evidence, which they hadn't taken to mean that they couldn't pursue fresh leads. They'd have to see what she thought about their brush with Speck and Pino.

If the expression on her face is any indication, we're in trouble, Joe thought as she strode into the room scowling. She was wearing a fleece jogging suit and no makeup. She ignored the count's outstretched hand and walked straight to Frank and Joe. "I had already planned to question you about your continued attempt to harass Signore Cafaggio," she said. "If you keep causing trouble like this, your father's reputation will not be able to prevent us from sending you back home."

"Now, look here, Inspector," the count said forcefully in English. "These boys have just been through quite a lot. I hope you have a good reason for treating them with such contempt. What's this about Antonio Cafaggio? We've already dealt with that episode, which was, I'm sorry to say, inspired by my daughter's rather unfortunate dislike of the man."

Joe thought Barducci seemed to be caught off guard by the count's defense of them. But what was she saying about what had happened earlier that evening? Had Pino, after he had been caught at the Boboli Gardens, identified them to the police? If so, what exactly had they been accused of? Had Cafaggio and Speck cooked up some story to deflect attention away from their operations, whatever they were?

At the end of Joe's attempt to sort it all out, all he

felt sure of was that Frank was right to have given him the keep-your-mouth-shut sign. He couldn't even be sure that the count, despite his current bout of friendliness, wasn't somehow involved, given his friendship with Cafaggio.

"I'm sorry, sir," Inspector Barducci said to the count after an awkward pause. "I must have misunderstood the nature of the complaint."

"Yes, indeed," the count said. "Because unless there's something I don't understand, these boys have acted courageously to uncover the very people you should be arresting."

"Perhaps so, sir, but Signore Cafaggio believes that they were checking on his business dealings with Mr. Speck when his assistant walked in."

"I see," the count said. "You boys didn't tell me it was Pino who chased you through the garden."

"We didn't think it mattered," Frank said, afraid of where this was leading. "It was Speck who pulled the gun on us."

"According to Mr. Speck," said the inspector, "he was only trying to protect his store—like Signore Cafaggio before him."

"And how do you explain the smoke bomb, Inspector?" the count asked.

"We've had them before—last month in the church in Colonnata. It's vandalism, plain and simple."

110

"What about the car that tried to run us over?" Joe asked.

"Many Americans complain of Italian drivers. They can be impetuous. Perhaps you were driving too carelessly and annoyed someone in a hurry."

The count shook his head, concerned. "I think we've had enough of this for now. Perhaps in the morning things will seem clearer. Thank you for coming, Inspector." He saw her to the door and then turned to the boys. "Since your room has been ruined, for whatever reason, I have arranged for you three to stay at a hotel in Colonnata. It will be safer there, as well. Stefano is waiting downstairs to drive you there."

The next morning Cosimo and the Hardys slept in and missed breakfast at the hotel, which was another grand old building with a past. The concierge told them where the best pasticceria in town was, and they walked down to the village square to find it.

"Not bad," Joe said after polishing off a shiny little air-filled pastry. "Now where's the food?"

They were standing up at the bar, next to a glass case filled with pastries on one side and sandwiches and small pizzas on the other. "Time to switch to lunch, I guess," Frank said, eyeing a pizza.

"I believe you Americans have poor eating habits," Cosimo said, calmly munching a plain piece of bread.

111

"If you say so, Cosimo," Joe said, joining Frank in front of the pizza section. "But my body needs more than air for breakfast."

"You should learn to control your body," Cosimo said. He was smiling, but Joe thought he wasn't kidding.

"You mean like those guys who walk over hot coals barefooted?" Joe asked.

"That would be an extreme case of what I mean, yes," Cosimo said, hesitating as though he thought he might be falling into a trap.

"I've got to admit, Cosimo," Joe said. "I'm not up to that level yet. I wouldn't even be able to sleep through your snoring without ear plugs. Good thing I brought some."

"Speaking of earplugs," Frank said, before Cosimo could reply, "I wish I had some now. Look who's coming."

"Oh great, Francesca's boyfriend, Vito," Joe said under his breath. "Have you met this jerk yet, Cosimo?"

Cosimo shook his head as Vito walked up next to Frank and barked an order to the man behind the bar. When he got his cappuccino, he turned to Frank and laughed. "Your face looks bad."

"Thanks, I know," Frank said. He wanted to say, "Your personality doesn't look too good, either," but he bit his tongue and hoped Vito would just leave.

Joe didn't see any point in beating around the bush. "Been hunting lately?" he asked Vito.

Vito glared at Joe with contempt. "I have better things to do, unlike you." He put down his coffee cup and walked out, throwing a bill in front of the cashier. Joe watched him strut out.

"And Francesca thinks she has good taste," Joe said, remembering her comment about Cafaggio's warehouse. "I'd rather have an ugly warehouse than that guy for a friend."

"Maybe he comes off better in Italian," Frank half-heartedly suggested. "We should have let Cosimo talk to him."

"That guy's a creep in any language—trust me," Joe said.

"I agree," Cosimo said. "Though Frank is right that some people's personalities do change when they switch languages."

"Yeah, I've noticed that Frank sounds kind of stupid in Italian."

"That's for sure," Cosimo agreed.

"All right, all right," Frank said as he watched Vito cross the piazza in front of the pasticceria. "The question is, why am I feeling so stupid in English right now? I can't get this case to make any sense. I almost feel that *everybody's* a suspect, but maybe that's just because I *am* stupid in Italian."

"I feel the same way," Cosimo admitted. "But then, I've never tried to be a detective."

Joe was still looking out the window as Vito turned toward the little church at the end of the street. "I'll be back in a second," he said, and quickly slipped out the door.

Joe stayed on the north side of the street and walked toward the church, keeping an eye on Vito. When Vito started to turn around, Joe ducked behind a car to avoid being spotted. At the small piazza between the post office and the church, Vito turned and took the footpath that led downhill through a small park. Joe crossed the street and walked over to the piazza, staying about fifty yards away from Vito. At the bottom of the park, there was a street lined with parked cars. Vito turned once more before stepping onto the pavement, and Joe quickly ducked behind a tree, not sure whether he'd been seen or not.

When Joe stepped away from the tree, he couldn't spot Vito. Then he heard a car start. He waited, then watched while a black sedan pulled out of its parking spot. Vito was in the driver's seat.

That's it! Joe said to himself. Vito must be the guy who tried to kill us!

12 Inspector Barducci

Joe had played out his hunch and hit pay dirt. Although he couldn't be absolutely positive this was the same car that had tried to run them down the night before, it was enough to put Vito on the list of suspects.

As he walked back to the pasticceria, Joe wondered about Francesca. It was possible that if Vito was involved in the theft, she didn't realize it. On the other hand, if Vito shot the rifle that spooked their horses—and if it was the same rifle they found in the secret chapel—then she had to know.

On second thought, Joe had to admit, it *was* possible that Francesca had shown Vito the secret chapel and Captain Ruffino's chest earlier, and that he had gone there on his own.

Joe walked back to the pasticceria feeling confused once again, though pretty positive that Vito had to be involved one way or another.

"So what did you do, Joe?" Cosimo asked as Joe walked up to the storefront. "Tell him to eat a better breakfast?"

"No, I figured the prison dietitian could take care of that."

Frank could see this was a serious joke, and he went a step further. "You followed him to his car, didn't you?"

"Yep."

"And it was the same one?"

"I think so. How did you guess?"

Joe looked at Frank and smiled. He shouldn't have been surprised that Frank had shadowed his every thought and move. That's what brothers are for. At least, that's what Frank seemed to be for.

"I think we were all thinking the same thing when Francesca wasn't in her room last night—that Vito had just picked her up in the car that tried to run us over. Then the smoke bomb distracted us," Frank explained.

"Which is what it was probably supposed to do," Cosimo added.

"And I guess Francesca would have to be a complete dope not to know what Vito has been up to," Joe advanced.

"I can see that it's *possible* for her not to know," Frank agreed. "She wasn't in the car when he chased us. And she was with us when the smoke bomb was thrown."

"She obviously didn't shoot the gun," Cosimo said. "And if Vito hid it in the secret chapel, it is possible that she didn't know, though she must have shown him the room to begin with."

"And the secret passage," added Joe.

"She might have shown him where she keeps the chloroform—if that's what she uses for her butter-flies—without knowing he was going to do anything with it," Frank continued.

"We still don't know whether Vito is involved with either Speck or Cafaggio," Joe said, straining hard to think if they knew anything that would link Vito to either man.

"I guess I assumed there was a link with Speck because we were run off the road just after our run-in with him," Frank said. "But maybe there's no connection."

"And now I'm wondering why Francesca sent us off to Signore Cafaggio's fort," Cosimo said.

"If she is part of this, she might have been trying to divert attention from Vito," Joe replied.

"Which would mean that she made up the story about her psychic," Frank said.

"And on the other hand," Cosimo countered, "the

story about the psychic could indicate that she is a gullible fool who really has no idea what is going on."

"Well, anyway," Frank said, "if we tell Inspector Barducci about Vito's car, she could search it and maybe his apartment for traces of the smoke bomb. Cosimo, do you mind calling her?"

Cosimo agreed and, after being put on hold a half-dozen times, eventually got through. He explained what they had figured out. Then Joe and Frank could see him nodding and saying "*Sì—sì, sì,*" during a long speech Barducci was giving him. He hung up the pay phone and looked downcast.

"What's wrong, Cosimo?" Joe asked.

"Basically, she told us to stop bothering her. She thinks we're imagining a lot of stuff. She says without a license plate number we can't know it was Vito. And even if he was driving dangerously close to you last night, he didn't actually hurt you. All it would prove is that he's a big jerk and he doesn't like you—which we already know."

"What about the fact that Francesca was gone when we went to her room last night?" Joe asked.

Cosimo shrugged and shook his head. "She has a right to take a walk—or go on a late-night ride with her boyfriend—and, unfortunately, the inspector herself has a butterfly collection." Cosimo paused. "I guess it doesn't exactly prove anything."

"You sound as if you've changed your mind," Frank said.

"I don't know," said Cosimo, gazing off toward the church. "I see the inspector's point about not having evidence. All we have are ideas, guesses. No reason to arrest—or even search—anybody."

"But she agrees that somebody at the villa must be involved to some extent, right? Who else would have known about the secret entrance?" Frank asked.

"Yes, she agrees with that," Cosimo said somberly. "And she seemed very interested in the rifle we found in the secret chapel."

"You told her about that?" Joe asked.

"Of course. It may be the only real piece of evidence we have—if it has prints on it. She was actually kind of mad we hadn't told her sooner."

"I guess Julia talked us out of that," Joe said.

"Speaking of Julia," Frank said, glancing up the hill toward the villa, "I guess our day off is just about up. You think we have time to try to check out where Vito lives before going back to the dig?"

"I suggest to wait until Inspector Barducci checks on the fingerprints," Cosimo said, using one of his slightly off patterns of speech.

"If we go back to the villa now, we could get ourselves a free lunch," Joe said.

"Now you are learning something," Cosimo said, patting Joe on the back as they set off for the villa.

"If it isn't the Three Musketeers," Julia said. She was just climbing out of the site when the boys arrived, and she looked as excited as she was hot and dirty. The photographer was packing up his camera, having just finished the daily shoot. "You won't believe what I've been finding while you guys were off battling evil. Come down and see."

Laid out neatly on the ground in a cluster about three feet from where the jewelry box had been were broken pieces of shaped stone. Joe could make out the hind legs of a horse in one fragment and a bearded human head in another. "Not bad, Julia," he said. "A couple of statues. You think they're important?"

"Extremely. But it's not two statues." She knelt down and moved a few pieces around. "You see how they fit together? It's a centaur—half man and half horse. The Etruscans loved fantastic beasts of all kinds, but this one, of course, shows a Greek influence."

"Of course," Joe said, putting on an English accent.

Julia smiled at Joe. "But what's significant about this is that the style shows no trace of Greek influence, despite its subject. You see how stylized the lines are—they're completely unnatural."

"Which is to say," Joe went on in the same exaggerated English accent, "that it looks nothing like a *real* centaur."

"You really are hopeless, Joe," she said affectionately as the lunch bell rang. "All right, now tell me what you gentlemen have been up to."

They began walking toward the dining hall for lunch, filling Julia in on all that had happened. When they rounded the hedge, Frank saw Inspector Barducci and another officer walking on the gravel path toward the lunchroom. The inspector briefly looked their way but kept walking until she and the officer were inside. Frank picked up the pace as they heard a man crying out emotionally in Italian, his voice echoing in the cavernous stone-walled room.

They all ran the thirty remaining yards toward the dining hall and arrived as the officers were escorting Bruno out of the door.

"*Sono innocente!*" Bruno cried repeatedly. I am innocent!

13 Francesca Goes Undercover

"Why Bruno?" Frank demanded, marching alongside Inspector Barducci.

The inspector kept walking at a fast clip toward the door that led from the garden to the street, while the other officer walked behind, prodding the hand-cuffed gardener along. She shot Frank a quick look and said curtly, as the count came walking up from the other direction, "Ask Count Ruffino." Then she and the officer dragged Bruno out. As he crossed the threshold, Bruno looked Frank in the eyes and said one more time, "*Sono innocente.*" I am innocent.

"I believe you boys will be safe now," the count said calmly after the door shut. "It's a pity about Bruno, though. I suppose the jewelry was too great a temptation."

"But how do you know he took it?" Joe asked, unable to believe the quick turn of events.

"I can't say for sure," he replied. "What I do know is that Bruno's fingerprints were all over my father's military rifle and that it had been fired recently. I had forgotten all about it until the inspector came about an hour ago to check the rifle."

"I see," Frank said, though he was actually quite confused. At one point he and Joe had wondered if Bruno was leading them on. The fact that he really had shouldn't have been such a surprise. But it was. Bruno didn't give Frank the feeling that he'd done anything but expertly tend the garden.

"In any case," continued the count, "the inspector had already considered Bruno her prime suspect because of his criminal record. And at the same time, a police informant has come forward as a witness against Bruno. So I'm afraid, all in all, it looks pretty bad for Bruno," the count concluded.

"Does Inspector Barducci think Bruno fired the rifle to scare our horses?" Frank asked.

"I believe that was it, yes."

"I see," Frank said again, though he felt no less confused. He knew that the cartridge that Joe had found—and still had—should be analyzed before assuming that it was fired by the 8-mm Mannlicher. Still, it didn't look good that Bruno had fired the gun at all, since he had denied ever seeing it. If he'd lied about that, he could well have lied about everything else.

"Well, I think it'll be all right for the boys to move back in, even though I still think Signore Cafaggio did it, Papa." Francesca had walked up during their conversation and was standing next to her father, her arm around his back. "And I can't believe Bruno would have tried to harm the Hardy brothers—or anyone."

"Now, now, *cara*—let's let the police do their jobs, shall we. And that applies to you, too, gentlemen."

"Francesca's a pretty convincing actress, if she's involved," Joe said after they had left the count and his daughter and walked into the dining hall. "I guess it's time to admit we messed up."

"I feel like saying Bruno was pretty convincing, too," Frank said. "But then I guess I can't really say that, since I never understand more than half of what he said. What do you think, Cosimo?"

"He fooled me. I thought he was a nice guy. And it seems as if he had a nice life here. It's a tragedy, really."

"It's sort of like that centaur you found, Julia," Joe said. "He looks like a nice guy, but he must really be kind of an animal who can't help himself."

"You've captured the myth perfectly, Joe. And to think that the man who maintained this beautiful garden was the thief. It's hard to take in."

"I don't know about you guys," Joe said after excavating all afternoon, "but I'm having trouble believing Bruno was responsible for all the things that have happened. Why would he take us into the secret chapel if he knew his fingerprints were on that rifle, and if he had used it to scare our horses?"

They were closing up the dig for the night, having found little of interest that afternoon. Julia had gone home early—exhausted, she had said, by all the excitement. "I agree," Cosimo said. "But then, he must have known his prints were on the gun. There isn't any way of planting phony fingerprints, is there?"

"Not any realistic way," Frank said. "Anyway, anybody trying to frame Bruno that way would have to know that somebody would find the gun. And who but Bruno knew he was going to show us the secret chapel? What I don't get is why Bruno pretended to have discovered the room when he had obviously been there before."

"I am afraid that there is only one solution," Cosimo announced as he began climbing up the ladder to ground level. "Bruno must have returned to the chapel after we left and handled the gun for some reason, perhaps out of simple curiosity. He probably obliterated the prints of the real thief."

Everyone agreed that Cosimo's theory made as much sense as any.

"So we've got to keep trying to figure this thing out," Joe said.

That night Joe had trouble sleeping. Another nightmare woke him up. He sat up and looked at the clock. Two in the morning. Quietly he got out of bed and slipped on his jeans and sandals. The moon was bright once again, so he decided to go for a walk in the garden. There, the croaking frogs kept him company as he strolled along the gravel paths, thinking. There was some thought that was lying below the surface of his conscious mind, but he couldn't bring it up.

Suddenly he remembered there would be guards on duty outside the dig site—Professor Mosca had insisted on two professionals. He realized he could easily startle them if he continued to walk around in the dark, so he decided to get onto the straight wide path that led to the site and walk slowly toward them while whistling. He'd been working on his Italian the past few days and thought he could have a bit of a conversation.

He was all ready to say *"Non posso dormire*—I can't sleep," when he got close enough to see the two guards slumped over on the ground. He raced to them and turned one of them over. He was breathing. So was the other one. Joe was about to leave them when he saw a small metallic object glittering in the moonlight on one of their backs. He bent down to take a closer look. An inch-long brass dart with a feathered quill was lodged in one of the men's dorsal muscles.

Joe ran back to his room and woke up Frank and Cosimo. "Come on, guys," he urged. "We've got to see if Francesca's in her room."

They all rushed over and pushed the door open. Joe turned the light on and saw that her bed was empty.

"Okay, that's it. I'm not going to let her wriggle out of this," Joe said. "Turn off the light and let's wait for her."

The next fifteen minutes felt like hours to Joe, but somehow he knew that Francesca would come back soon. She was probably helping Vito stash the statue—or whatever they had stolen—somewhere safe. Or maybe they were delivering it to their dealer. He wondered what they would be pulling next, now that they had graduated to dart guns.

Finally the door opened. Frank switched on the light, and Francesca tried to run. Joe jumped up and

127

tackled her. She kicked him hard in the stomach and scrambled to her feet. Joe recovered soon enough to snag her left foot and send her reeling. He got up and grabbed her firmly by the arm. She struggled for a few seconds and then gave up. Joe pulled her into the bedroom and shut the door.

"We know about everything, Francesca," Joe said. "If you help us catch Vito, you might be able to reduce your sentence."

"You're not the police," she scoffed. "You can't make deals like that."

"Okay, then, we'll just take you in right now, and Vito will have a nice life without you on the French Riviera."

She pursed her lips for a second and then said, "All right. I'll help."

Frank, who had been sleeping soundly only twenty minutes earlier, couldn't believe what was happening. "What made you do it, Francesca? Wasn't five million dollars enough for you."

"You don't understand," she said, crying. "Speck made us do it. He said he wouldn't pay us at all until we got him something else. And if we refused, he said he would have Papa killed." She sobbed again.

"So it *is* Speck," said Joe. "Look, Francesca, I'm sure if you help us catch Speck, it'll help. Do you know what happens next, or is Vito in charge now?"

"He's . . . he's always been in charge," cried Francesca. "He talked me into it . . . I thought I could save the estate. . . ."

"Okay, okay, just try to remember what Vito said he would do next," Joe said.

"He's going to meet Speck in front of the church in Colonnata to make the transfer," she explained. "They were going to meet at three-thirty this morning."

"That's in a half hour," Frank pointed out. "We've got to act fast."

"How about if Francesca shows up with that secret recording device you brought," Cosimo suggested, "and gets Speck to talk about the thefts?"

"Brilliant, Cosimo," Joe said. "But how's she going to explain suddenly showing up. Speck won't like that."

"Maybe Francesca could say she's worried that the police have planted a homing device on the statue," Frank said.

"Let's try it," Joe said. "Do you think you can pull it off, Francesca?"

"I . . . I think so," she said weakly.

They sneaked quietly out of the family apartment, and then Joe ran to get the wire from their room. After taping the miniature transmitter to Francesca's stomach, everyone started to get into Francesca's car. Suddenly Cosimo pulled back. "Perhaps it would be better to call Inspector Barducci at this point. Speck is a dangerous man."

"There's no time," Frank said, but he could see that Cosimo was scared stiff. "You're right, though, Cosimo, about the inspector. Do you mind staying behind and calling her?"

"No, not at all," Cosimo said, obviously relieved. "You guys be careful."

On the short ride, Frank and Joe decided that they would get out before reaching the piazza. Then they would hold the receiver and tape recorder at a safe distance, while Francesca would proceed to drive to the piazza. That way, if Speck got suspicious and checked the car, he wouldn't find anything.

After getting dropped off, Frank and Joe took a back alley to a spot behind the post office where they could watch without being seen.

"Something's going wrong," Joe whispered as he strained to see into the dimly lit piazza. He had on the headset and was listening in on what was being said.

"Did they spot the wire on Francesca?" asked Frank. He could see Speck giving instructions to two athletic-looking men in dark suits. They were standing beside a limousine next to Francesca and Vito.

"No. Speck's saying he's glad she showed up, so that he can get rid of both of them at once."

Frank and Joe crouched down and watched while the men shoved Francesca and Vito into the trunk of the limo and then quickly got into the front seat. Speck scanned the piazza before getting in, and then the limo drove quietly away.

14 Dishonor Among Thieves

Joe took off his headset and watched the limo climb the steep road leading out of town. He memorized the license plate number even though he had a feeling it wouldn't do any good. Cosimo was probably having as much trouble as before getting hold of Inspector Barducci. At any rate, there were no police cars in sight. It looked as though there was nothing they could do to save Francesca and Vito.

"What if we start knocking on doors until somebody agrees to call the police," Joe proposed in desperation.

"I don't think so," Frank said. "It's the middle of the night. They'd probably have *us* arrested."

"At least the cops would come," Joe countered.

"And do you think we could explain the real problem without Cosimo?"

"How about if we hot-wire Francesca's car and chase the limo?" Joe offered.

"We don't have any tools, Joe."

"Maybe she's got some in the trunk."

"I don't know," Frank replied. "We'd probably just waste a lot of time and not get anywhere."

"If something happens to Francesca, it'll be our fault," Joe said grimly.

"I think our only option is to run back to the villa. Cosimo can explain the crisis to the police or the *carabinieri,*" Frank said, referring to the Italian military police. "At this time of night, with hardly any other cars out, they might be able to track down the limo from the air."

"Okay, let's go!" Joe said. He threw down his eavesdropping equipment, and they started running the two miles to the villa. They made it up to the house with the horse trough and turned the corner.

Suddenly bright lights from a car filled the air and blinded them. Before they could run away, Speck's men, one blond and the other with jet black hair, were using the barrels of their submachine guns to shove them toward the limo, which was idling in the middle of the street.

Frank was pushed into the backseat first. He looked up and saw Vito grinning at him. Francesca was sitting on his right. She looked the other way as Vito began laughing. "You like our show?" he asked as Joe was flung in beside Frank. "You must have felt so *sorry* for Francesca." He laughed and put an arm around Francesca. "Look how clever is Francesca." He took out a piece of paper, unfolded it, and handed it to Frank.

" *'Fratelli Hardy stanno guardando.'* " Frank read it out loud. "The Hardy brothers are watching," Francesca had written. She must have handed it to Vito before the Hardys had arrived at the piazza. The "show" must have been planned out on paper, too, so that the bug wouldn't pick it up. Francesca was getting the last laugh after all.

Speck turned around in the front seat as the limo sped off. He looked relaxed and pleased with himself. "Well, it's been quite an adventure, boys, but I think we'll do the Swiss leg of the trip without you. Any last requests before we find a nice place to, ah, put you?"

"Just tell me how you're going to explain Francesca's disappearance," Frank said.

"Oh, how careless of me!" Speck replied. "You're absolutely right, Mr. Hardy. We *must* stop and swing back to the villa to drop off Francesca. Then she can explain everything to the police. Splendid plan, indeed!" He laughed, as the limo turned onto the wide road at the base of the hill, apparently on its way to the *autostrada* that went north to Bologna and eventually to Switzerland.

"What are we going to do about Cosimo, Mr. Speck?" Francesca asked, apparently having realized for the first time that there was a problem in her scheme to double-cross the Hardys. "I'm afraid he knows about you."

"I see. Well, now, that *does* seem inconvenient, doesn't it?"

"No one will listen to the boy," Vito said.

"Well, it doesn't really matter to me," said Speck. "No one will have any evidence connecting me to any of this."

"Francesca won't ever be able to go home, will she?" Frank asked. "She'll be a fugitive for the rest of her life."

Frank watched Francesca stiffen, as though she had just realized that he was right. "You'll never get away with this!" she shouted. "My father will have you hunted down."

"It's a little late to worry about that now, don't you think, *cara*? Besides, it's not so bad being a fugitive—is it, Claudio?" Speck looked at Vito and smiled. Vito—or was it Claudio?—shrugged and said, "I feel more free than before."

Francesca slumped back in her seat and buried her face in her hands. She seemed to be in a state of shock. Frank almost felt sorry for her, but he couldn't help thinking that she deserved to find out that she'd been dating a fugitive con man.

"You mean you guys set this whole thing up way in advance, including getting Francesca to fall for Vito?" Joe asked.

"It wasn't quite so precise as all that," said Speck. "You plant seeds, and some turn into beautiful flowers. I never thought this one would be so easy to pick, did you, Claudio?"

"I had a good feeling," he said, laughing cruelly as he watched Francesca sobbing.

"But, of course," Speck continued, "if the dig hadn't turned up anything, we would have found some other flowers to pick in that lovely villa. My foolish friend Antonio Cafaggio has described many of them to me."

So that was it, Frank finally realized. Speck and Claudio had been preparing to rob the villa, not the Etruscan site. When the jewelry box showed up, they just made a slight adjustment in their plans. But there was one thing that didn't make any sense.

"Why did you let Francesca in on the robbery?" Frank asked. "You wouldn't have us to worry about right now if you hadn't."

"Well done, young man!" Speck said enthusiastically. "You have hit on a flaw in our operation. We hadn't counted on Francesca being such a sly little thing, had we, *cara?*"

Francesca had stopped sobbing and was glaring at Speck. "It didn't take a genius to see what you two were up to."

"But it *would* have taken a genius to outsmart us," Speck said. "And I'm afraid you fell short on that score."

"Wait a minute," Joe said to Francesca. "You mean, you figured out these guys were going to rob you and you didn't turn them in?"

"I couldn't," she replied. "Speck threatened to have Papa killed if I told the police. So I agreed to work with them, but only in return for a cut in the profits. That way, Papa would collect the insurance money for the stolen goods, and I would get half as much again from the black-market sale. I would have saved the villa—if you two hadn't gotten in the way."

"How were you going to explain the money to your father?" Frank asked.

"With his experience in forgery, Speck was going to manufacture an inheritance from some long-lost cousin," Francesca explained. "And the money was going to go into a Swiss bank account."

"You fell for that?" Joe said to Francesca. "You never would have seen that money."

"You see what I mean about Francesca not being a genius," Speck said, laughing.

"But why were you so surprised just now to find

that Vito, or Claudio, is a con man?" Frank asked Francesca. He was beginning to feel sorry for her.

"He convinced me that Speck was threatening him, just like me—and that he had met me before Speck." She looked contemptuously at Claudio. "I thought we were in this together."

"Poor Francesca," Speck snarled. "She thinks she's the only one with a good reason to be dishonest. It's a failing common in our trade, I'm afraid."

The limo had traveled about fifteen minutes on the *autostrada* when the driver pulled off and took a narrow road that led into a forest.

"I'm afraid there's been a slight change in plans, children," Speck said as the car stopped and the two armed men jumped out to open the back doors. "I think you'll all be happier together, don't you? You, too, Claudio, get out."

Joe, who had been sitting on the edge of the backseat, with Frank between him and Claudio, had managed to take off his belt during the ride without anyone's noticing. It was a western-style belt with a heavy metal buckle. When the blond thug opened the door and pointed the gun at him, Joe got out peacefully, but as Frank was getting out, Joe swung the buckle forcefully down on the man's hand.

The gun fell to the ground, and Frank lunged for it. As he was about to reach it, the man stomped on his hand. Joe leaped onto him, grabbing him around the upper body and pulling him off balance. Frank was about to grab the gun when he heard Claudio behind him, yelling, "Stop—hands up!" They turned around to see Claudio holding the machine gun in one hand and the black-haired thug's arm in the other.

Frank and Joe put their hands up, and as the blond thug slowly got up, Frank could see Speck slide over in the front seat of the limo and grab the steering wheel. Before Claudio could react, the car had peeled off into the night. Claudio shot after it without causing it to stop, cursing at Speck in Italian.

Claudio threw the black-haired thug to the ground and reached down to retrieve the other gun. "Okay, everybody walk over behind those trees," he said, pointing both guns. "No one will be able to see you there from the road."

"What good will it do *you*, Claudio, to kill us?" Joe asked. Joe didn't know if that was Claudio's plan or not, but he knew from his experience with criminals in hostage situations that it's always better to keep them talking.

Claudio remained silent as everyone, including the two thugs, walked reluctantly into the woods. Frank tried to draw him out. "You know, if you help the police find Speck, you might be able to work out a good deal for yourself." Frank didn't know how the

Italian criminal justice system worked, but he had to try something.

"You forget I am already a fugitive. I have nothing to gain by being caught. Besides, I plan on catching Speck myself. Then he will wish that the police had caught him!"

"So what good will it do to kill us?"

"I have not yet decided what to do with you, but if you don't shut up, I *will* kill you for sure."

Now the group was in a small opening in the thick stand of trees, about fifty yards from the road. "You boys tie the men's hands behind their backs with their belts," he said.

Frank and Joe did what he said, tying the thugs' hands together.

"Now you," he said, pointing to Joe. "Tie Francesca to your brother."

Joe did so.

"Now lie down on your stomach."

Joe did as he said.

Frank watched in horror as Claudio slowly walked over to Joe, pointing the gun at him.

Francesca screamed, "No!"

15 The Truth at Last

Frank sat on the forest floor, his hands fastened to Francesca's, and watched helplessly as Claudio—if that was his real name—approached Joe. He was starting to aim at Joe's back when Francesca screamed once more. Claudio looked over at her and said something in Italian. It was the first time Frank or Joe had heard him use his native tongue. His words came out in a fast staccato, with a strange pronunciation that neither Frank nor Joe had heard before. But Francesca came back with a torrent of words that seemed to silence him.

Claudio lowered his gun to his side. "If you come after me, I'll kill you," he said to Joe. Without saying goodbye to Francesca, he ran toward the road and was soon out of sight.

Joe got up and untied Frank and Francesca. By the diffuse blue-gray morning light, Joe watched the thugs get to their feet and struggle to loosen their bound hands. "Not so fast," he said, realizing that they probably didn't understand English. Not that they would have listened.

They began running away slowly and awkwardly since they were still joined at the hands. Frank and Joe together jumped on their backs and wrestled them to the ground. Then Joe tried to hold them down while Frank got the other belt to tie their legs with.

The plan didn't work. The thugs kept kicking and squirming, and it looked as if they were about to free their hands when Francesca came up and grabbed both of the thugs by the hair, pulling them back down to the ground. They screamed as she pulled hard, and then they finally submitted to being tied up with a belt.

After they were secured, Francesca stood up, put her hands together, and lifted them toward Frank. "My turn," she said.

"There aren't any belts left," Frank said. "You walk ahead of us."

As the sun pushed back the night, they walked silently toward the *autostrada,* into a light breeze. Frank watched the wind ruffle Francesca's dark curls, and he remembered following her on horseback and thinking that she belonged there on that mountain, her hair bouncing to the same rhythm as Lola's mane. Now he wondered if she would ever be able to ride there again.

When they reached the highway, a gas station was just opening for business.

"I guess the fastest way to reach the police at this point is to call the villa," Frank said as they approached the tasteful stone building.

"I bet by now Cosimo has led them to the recording device," said Joe.

"Which means they'll have a pretty good idea of what actually happened," said Frank, looking at Francesca as she blankly watched the cars zipping by on the *autostrada*. "Count Ruffino probably thinks Francesca's dead by now."

Upon hearing this, Francesca took off toward the highway and screamed, "I wish I *were* dead!" They ran after her and caught her. She didn't try to fight their grip as they slowly led her back to the gas station.

Joe let go of her and handed her over to Frank. "I'll go make the call," he said.

After standing in silence for several minutes, Frank ventured a word. "If we hadn't caught you, you would never have seen Claudio again. You would have been robbed blind. No payment, no boyfriend."

Francesca nodded and kept looking down. She

didn't seem to mind hearing Frank laying it all out for her, so he went on.

"Now at least you know you were tricked by professionals. They've probably done stuff like this before. Of course, it doesn't really excuse you. You agreed to steal the artifacts."

Apparently having heard enough, she turned away from Frank. "Those things had been on our family estate for centuries. They belong to us."

"Give it up, Francesca." Frank couldn't believe that anybody could be so piggishly selfish as to really think that. "Those things are way too important to belong to one family," he said. "Julia said that nothing's ever been found like those jewels. Besides, your family hasn't owned the land for two and a half thousand years. In the big scheme of history, you're a newcomer—and a spoiled one at that."

That was the end of the discussion. When Joe came out, they let her sit by herself on a bench until the police came.

They got Francesca to direct the police to the spot where they had tied up the thugs. But the police seemed reluctant to believe her. Then they were all shoved roughly into the backseat of one of the two squad cars.

"I guess they don't know whom to trust," Frank said.

"Can't blame them, exactly," Joe said. "I'm just starting to get a grip on all this myself."

"Let's hope the dynamic duo is still tied up. I think the police will believe us if they see we bagged those guys."

There were a few tense minutes while Frank and Joe waited in the car for the police to find the thugs. "Whew!" Joe said as the two were led out of the woods.

When the men had been secured in the back of the other car, both cars set off for Florence. After a few exchanges on the police radio, the officer in the front passenger seat turned around and gave Frank and Joe a smile. *"Avete fato bene,"* he said.

Francesca explained what she had gleaned from the radio conversation. "The men have been identified. They both have long records," she said flatly. "It looks like you two will be big heroes at the police station in Florence."

"We're not going to Sesto Fiorentino?" Joe asked.

"No, it sounds like they're bringing in all kinds of agents from different departments to question you. They've also notified all the border crossings so they can catch Speck."

Soon after they arrived at the station, they heard that Speck had been picked up on the *autostrada* long before he arrived at the Swiss border. He had both the statue of the centaur and the jewelry box with him, along with several other stolen artifacts.

Inspector Barducci arrived after they'd already been interrogated by agents from customs and from the organized crime unit centered in Rome, all of whom spoke perfect English. Francesca had stayed with them and confessed everything willingly.

"I suppose I owe you gentlemen an apology," the inspector said after consulting with the agents.

"That's okay," Joe said. "It turns out we didn't have a very good idea of what was going on, anyway."

"You were way ahead of me." She turned to Francesca. "Now, young lady, what are we going to do with you?"

They began speaking in Italian, while Frank and Joe were told they were free to go. An officer came in holding a large cardboard box and offered them a ride back to the villa.

"I think the archaeologists will be glad to see you bringing this back."

"You've got the artifacts?" Frank asked excitedly.

"Yes, well, I saw one piece of jewelry my wife would like, but in general it is a little too, uh . . ."

"Old-fashioned?" Joe supplied, while the officer searched for the right word in English.

"Yes, that's it," he said, laughing.

By the time the police dropped Frank and Joe back at the villa, it was midafternoon. At that point, there was still no word on who Vito, a.k.a. Claudio, might be. He was still on the loose, and Frank and Joe figured he might be hard to catch.

Cosimo and Julia were sitting on the bench under the statue of Hercules and Cerberus when the Hardys entered the garden with the box. Frank and Joe sneaked up on them from behind.

"A package for Julia Russell!" Joe announced as he put the box down on the bench next to her.

"No!" she screamed in delight. "It can't be!"

"With our compliments," Frank said.

"We couldn't get the police to tell us anything," Cosimo said as Julia opened the box. "What happened?"

"Never mind!" Julia cried. "Look at this, will you. The jewelry is more beautiful than I remembered."

Once the excitement died down a little, they exchanged stories, and Cosimo explained that he and the count had gone to the piazza with the police at about four in the morning. They had stayed in Inspector Barducci's car while five other police cars converged on the scene where Francesca and "Vito" had put on their show. By the time they arrived, the place was deserted. When they found the eavesdropping equipment that Joe had thrown on the ground, everyone assumed that Frank and Joe had been discovered, even though the tape didn't reveal anything about how it had happened.

The whole business had been very hard on the count, but when he heard the tape of his daughter being thrown in the trunk and threatened with death, he was beside himself.

"It was terrible to watch the poor man," said Cosimo. "He kept blaming himself for doing a bad job raising Francesca after his wife died."

"From what you say," Julia said, "it's actually pretty hard to know what to make of Francesca. She certainly did wrong, but she was also the victim of some very treacherous people. I guess she's young enough to have learned a lesson."

"Speaking of which, has anybody seen Bruno?" Frank asked. "It sure is good to know that he wasn't the thief."

"He came back earlier today," Cosimo pointed out. "And you will be glad to know that my theory was exactly right."

"You mean, he went back to the gun and fooled around with it?" Joe asked.

"Yes. He said he was just curious."

"Boy, we're going to have to give him a hard time about that," Frank said.

"No kidding," Joe said. "If we'd found Vito's fingerprints on that gun, this whole thing would have been over much earlier."

"Except that Julia convinced us not to do anything about the gun," Frank pointed out, smiling at Julia.

"I thought you were just a couple of silly boys with delusions of grandeur. I still can't believe that you pulled this off."

"And what about now?" Joe asked.

"Hmm. No, you're right. *Silly* must not be the right word." Julia smiled as she looked them over thoroughly. "Let's see now—there's Frank, with a big scab across his face, his belt missing, and ridiculously dirty clothes."

"Never mind," Joe said. "You can skip my description."

"No, really, Joe, I do concede that *silly* was the wrong word, but I can't think of the right one."

"How about *humbled*," Joe suggested.

"Okay, good, that'll do," Julia said. "After all, I wouldn't want any of this to go to your head. We've still got work to do."

THE HARDY BOYS® SERIES By Franklin W. Dixon

LOOK FOR AN EXCITING NEW
HARDY BOYS MYSTERY COMING FROM
MINSTREL® BOOKS

NANCY DREW® MYSTERY STORIES By Carolyn Keene

A MINSTREL® BOOK

Published by Pocket Books

TAKE A RIDE
WITH THE KIDS ON BUS FIVE!

Natalie Adams and James Penny have just started
third grade. They like their teacher, and they like
Maple Street School. The only trouble is, they have
to ride bad old Bus Five to get there!

#1 THE BAD NEWS BULLY
Can Natalie and James stop the bully on Bus Five?

#2 WILD MAN AT THE WHEEL
When Mr. Balter calls in sick,
the kids get some strange new drivers.

#3 FINDERS KEEPERS
The kids on Bus Five keep losing things.
Is there a thief on board?

#4 I SURVIVED ON BUS FIVE
Bad luck turns into big fun
when Bus Five breaks down in a rainstorm.

BY MARCIA LEONARD
ILLUSTRATED BY JULIE DURRELL

 A MINSTREL BOOK

Published by Pocket Books

1237-04